Madiso...
heavy-...
it, too...

This urging, yearning to be joined.

Jake's eyes danced with inherent naughtiness and when he dropped his backpack, she dropped hers. Then he slowly stripped off his black T-shirt and when she got a good look at his honed, muscled chest, her heart slammed into her rib cage.

"C'mere," he murmured.

In a dreamlike state, Madison moved toward him, pulled by a force she didn't understand and could not resist.

He slipped his arms around her, pulled her down on the grass in the clearing, kissed her tenderly as if she were as rare and precious as the orchids around them.

Madison's cell phone rang, the sound echoing in the forest.

"Your friends," he said. "What about the bet?"

She crawled across the grass, fumbled for the cell in her backpack, answered it and gasped, "I'm out."

Blaze

Dear Reader,

Normally my Blaze heroines are rather inexperienced and looking to stretch their sexual wings, but with *Sweet Surrender,* I asked myself, what if there was a group of friends who'd all had their hearts broken the previous summer and swore this year would be different? What if they even made a bet that they could stay celibate during their summer vacations? That's how the idea for this book was born. Four friends, three stories, no sex on their vacations, winner take all.

In the first novella we travel to sexy Rio de Janeiro with Bianca St. James as her job puts her in close quarters with playboy Thomaz Santos. The second novella features brainy, introverted Madison Garrett who's certain she's going to win the bet in the jungles of Costa Rica. What she doesn't count on is gorgeous orchid thief Jake Strickland…who will stop at nothing to get what he wants. Then it's down to Emma. But what she's surprised by is sexy wilderness guide Trent Colton—the one who once got away. The same guy who's now sending Emma sizzling looks over the campfire underneath the Colorado night sky.

I hope you enjoy *Sweet Surrender.* And don't forget to check out all the other great Blaze novels available this month.

Much love,

Lori

Lori Wilde

SWEET SURRENDER

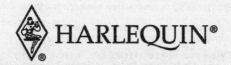

TORONTO • NEW YORK • LONDON
AMSTERDAM • PARIS • SYDNEY • HAMBURG
STOCKHOLM • ATHENS • TOKYO • MILAN • MADRID
PRAGUE • WARSAW • BUDAPEST • AUCKLAND

ISBN-13: 978-0-373-79565-9

SWEET SURRENDER

www.eHarlequin.com

Printed in U.S.A.

ABOUT THE AUTHOR

Lori Wilde is the author of forty books. She's been nominated for a RITA® Award and four *RT Book Reviews* Reviewers' Choice Awards. Her books have been excerpted in *Cosmopolitan, Redbook* and *Quick & Simple*. Lori teaches writing online through Ed2go. She's also an R.N. trained in forensics, and she volunteers at a women's shelter. Visit her Web site at www.loriwilde.com.

Books by Lori Wilde

HARLEQUIN BLAZE
  30—A TOUCH OF SILK
  66—A THRILL TO REMEMBER
106—PACKED WITH PLEASURE
123—AS YOU LIKE IT
152—GOTTA HAVE IT
175—SHOCKINGLY SENSUAL
230—ANGELS AND OUTLAWS*
260—DESTINY'S HAND*
346—MY SECRET LIFE**
399—CROSSING THE LINE†
411—SECRET SEDUCTION†
423—LETHAL EXPOSURE†
463—THE RIGHT STUFF††
506—ZERO CONTROL
518—HIS FINAL SEDUCTION

*The White Star
**The Martini Dares
†Perfect Anatomy
††Uniformly Hot!

Don't miss any of our special offers. Write to us at the following address for information on our newest releases.

Harlequin Reader Service
U.S.: 3010 Walden Ave., P.O. Box 1325, Buffalo, NY 14269
Canadian: P.O. Box 609, Fort Erie, Ont. L2A 5X3

To my most loyal Blaze reader, Laurie N.
Thank you so much for reading.

Prologue

Once upon a time there were four sexy single women in the city looking for love in all the wrong places...

"A MODERN-DAY chastity belt? You gotta be freakin' kidding me." Izzy Montgomery hooted and stabbed her fingers, adorned with numerous rings, through a mass of loose blond curls. "You've got the coolest job in the world, B."

"Well," said Bianca St. James, "it's not so much a chastity belt as a sex toy." She and her three best friends, Izzy, Emma and Madison, had met for their last girls' night out before they all dispersed to various parts of the globe for their summer holidays. Bianca's trip was more of a working vacation. But then again, she'd never had a *vacation,* vacation and that's the way she liked it. She didn't know what to do with herself when she wasn't working.

They were dining at Jackdaw's, midtown Manhattan's latest "hot spot." Izzy had picked the restaurant. Trust her to go for loud, flashy and overpriced.

Accompanied by the throbbing beat of hip music from the sound system, they'd already slurped down a pitcher of pomegranate martinis and noshed their way through pan-seared black truffles and quail grilled with an orange fennel glaze. They were all feeling a little tipsy and making fun of the item sitting in the middle of the table.

Everyone that is, except for Bianca. She'd expected jokes, yes. But this was her livelihood, and she took it very seriously, even if the product in question was of a frivolous nature.

"So honestly, would you buy this? And if not, what would make you buy it?" Bianca asked, trying to keep them on task. She held up the silky lingerie fitted with a GPS tracking device and an electronic sensor that measured the body temperature and pulse rate of the wearer.

The lingerie came as a set that included a lace bodice, sexy string-bikini bottoms and a faux pearl belt where the body temperature sensor was sewn in. The tiny GPS device lay nestled against the waist in the gossamer part of the see-through bodice. This model was purple and white, but it came in four different colors.

Madison tilted her head and looked over the top of her snazzy red-framed spectacles, eying the garment with studious intent. She had coal-black hair and smooth porcelain skin. She'd make a perfect Goth girl, but she was simply a total brainiac with a sharp appreciation for heavy-duty sunscreen. "No way. I sleep in T-shirts and boy shorts. That thing would cramp my style."

"The point of this…um…*thing*," Izzy interjected, "has nothing to do with sleeping and everything to do with sex."

"Or the lack thereof," Emma added.

Emma took the last bite of quail from the communal appetizer plate and dabbed at her mouth with a napkin. With her petite frame and soft, caramel-colored curly hair that fell to her waist, in the dim lighting—and through the haze of a couple of pomegranate martinis—Emma looked as if she could have stepped out of a renaissance painting. Although she had an Austen-like belief in romantic love.

"What woman would get that for herself?" Madison arched her ebony eyebrows. "It's something an insecure guy gives to his woman because he's terrified she's going to cheat on him."

"A girl would only buy that if she was in a relationship," Emma said. "It's not like the undies come with handcuffs, Mace and a rottweiler to fend off attackers."

"It's not really a modern-day chastity belt," Bianca re-iterated, gently trying to steer them back to her question before they got sidetracked by rottweilers or something equally off-topic, as their conversations tended to do on girls' night outs. "That's only what naysayers have dubbed it, and because of the misleading nickname, people have gotten the wrong idea about the Catch Me if You Can lingerie line. In Brazil the product is jumping off the shelves, but our billionaire client is upset by dismal US sales and he's hired Stillman, Burke and Hollister to find out how we can change the trend. Hence my bit of marketing research with three potential customers in our target demographic— single, young, urban professionals."

"If you threw in an *R* word, you'd have the acronym SYRUP," said Madison, who loved word games.

"Randy," Izzy readily supplied. "Single, young, *randy,* urban professionals. We're syrups."

"Speak for yourself," Emma muttered. "If I never have sex again it will be too soon." She was in the dumps because the guy she'd been dating on and off since their hot fling on a Greek cruise the previous summer had abruptly broken things off with her and gotten engaged to a woman who was Emma's polar opposite.

Izzy slung an arm around Emma's shoulders. "Ryan

was a jerk, okay? I didn't want to say anything at the time because you really seemed to be into him, but he was cruel to string you along. At least my summer fling told me right off the bat he was only interested in sex. That way, I didn't get emotionally invested."

"You never get emotionally invested," Bianca pointed out.

Izzy waved a hand and took the last swallow of her martini. "That's beside the point."

"It's precisely the point," Emma argued.

Izzy ignored her and reached out to stroke the glamorous lingerie Bianca passed over to her. "So tell us about the dude from Brazil who came up with this thing."

"You're letting your fantasies run away with you," Madison said. "Chances are he's old and wrinkled or he likes men."

Izzy raised an eyebrow. "Whoever designed this lovely piece of fluff definitely likes women. Look at the detail in the cup of the bra and the expert stitching." She switched her gaze to Bianca. "Is he hot?"

"Thomaz Santos?"

"Is he the designer?"

"Yes. He is young, however, only thirty-one. He inherited his grandmother's swimwear company and he's branching out into lingerie."

"Thomaz Santos," Madison mused. "Where have I heard that name?"

"Polo," Emma said. "He used to play at a professional level and from what I've heard, he's also something of an international jet-setting playboy."

They all looked at her and said in unison, "How do you know that?"

She shrugged. "Ryan was a polo enthusiast."

"Don't get started on him again," Izzy said to Emma,

and then remarked to Bianca, "This is quite promising indeed. Rich and powerful and clearly a master of a woman's body—"

"And he's a spoiled playboy," Bianca said. "Not my type. You know how I feel about men who've had everything handed to them."

Izzy covered her ears. "Yeah, yeah, you have no use for guys who didn't have to scratch and claw their way to the top. You're a reverse snob. You do know that, don't you?"

Okay, so Bianca did have a prejudice against rich, lazy, immature men who lived off family money. She wasn't going to deny it. Bianca had a nose-to-the-grindstone work ethic. She set a high standard, both for herself and others, and she wasn't going to apologize for it.

"I hear that in Brazil," Izzy said, adding a phony Latin accent to the last word, pronouncing it Braaazil. "The men are *muy macho*."

"That's Spanish," Bianca corrected. "In Brazil they speak Portuguese."

"Really?" Izzy looked surprised.

"Why do you think my company put me on the account?" Bianca asked. "I'm the only one at the agency who speaks Portuguese."

On Monday, Bianca's boss had called her into his office to give her the account she'd been working toward her entire career. If she could make a success of Thomaz Santos's lingerie in America, she'd be in line for a promotion to head of marketing, making her the youngest female department head in the history of Stillman, Burke and Hollister. Just thinking about it made her shiver. And the opportunity was due to the fact she had Brazilian blood running through her veins. *Way to go, Mom*. Bianca had to remember to give her mom a big kiss when she saw her on Sunday to thank her for being born in Brazil and making sure Bianca knew how to speak Portuguese.

But her boss had also made it clear that if there was a repeat performance of what had happened to her the previous summer, not only would she not get the promotion, she'd lose her job. It was a test, really. To see if she'd shored up her flaws. Remembering the Big Mistake of last summer sent a flush of embarrassment running though her.

But they were giving her a second chance. They were sending her to Brazil for however long she needed to nail the account. Santos Enterprises was their largest and most lucrative new client, and her firm was banking on this campaign leading to more business in Brazil and South America.

"So how do you say *muy macho* in Portuguese?" Izzy asked.

"*Muito macho.*"

Izzy rolled her eyes. "Oh, it's *so* the same thing."

"The difference may be subtle, but it's important," Bianca said.

"That makes me want a mojito." Emma hiccuped and then giggled.

"No more alcohol for you," Bianca warned. "Ryan's not worth the price of a hangover."

"Besides, mojitos are Cuban." Izzy shifted in her seat.

"In French," Madison added, apropos of nothing. "It's *très male.*"

"In Italian it's *molto maschio,*" Emma piped up.

"Show-offs, the lot of you. Not everyone could afford to go to college and study foreign languages." Izzy pretended to pout.

She might be teasing in that devil-may-care way of hers, but street-savvy Izzy had come up the hard way and she'd never let her lack of a formal education stop her. After years of struggling, she was finally gaining the reputation she deserved as a syndicated cartoonist.

Bianca was so proud of her. Personally, she'd put herself through college, working two jobs and still graduating with a 3.8 GPA, but she knew not everyone was as driven to succeed as she was, and Izzy had come from a truly impoverished background. "Yes, but how many people can say they make a living as a cartoonist? You're one of only a handful of people in the world."

"You do have a point. My cartoon alter ego, Cherry, gets to do everything I don't, including owning a summerhouse in the Hamptons. So." Izzy propped her elbow on the table and rested her chin in her palm. "Back to the guy. Do you suppose Thomaz Santos is *muito macho?* He sounds like he's *muito macho.* Maybe I could use him as a new love interest for Cherry."

Bianca snapped her fingers. "Forget about the guy for a minute and concentrate on the lingerie. What could provoke you to buy it?"

"Let me get this straight so I can make an informed comment." Madison pushed her plate aside, sat back and looped her elbow over the arm of her chair. As the scientific one in the group, she was always the first to apply analysis and logic to a topic. "This tiny bit of lingerie comes equipped with a vital-signs sensor and GPS tracking. So if you're getting all hot and bothered, your lover will know what's going on with your body and come looking for you with a sexual tryst in mind?"

"Exactly." Bianca nodded.

"What if he doesn't come looking?" Izzy asked.

"Then I guess he's just not all that into you." Madison canted her head.

"Or what if he comes after you and catches you with someone else?" Emma asked breathlessly.

"Why are you worried about that?" Izzy snorted. "You're loyal to a fault."

"I'm just asking on general principle," Emma retorted, "and maybe I've just decided loyalty is for the birds."

"Well, there's the rub," Bianca interjected. "That's why some people are calling it a modern-day chastity belt. But in reality, all a woman has to do is turn off the device if she doesn't want to be found. It's really about sex games, like Izzy said, not preserving one's chastity."

"But you could use it that way," Izzy postulated. "If you wanted."

"I suppose."

"How much does it cost?" Madison inquired.

"She's always so practical." Emma shook her head.

"Which is why she has money in her savings account and we don't." Izzy passed the lingerie to Madison.

"Two hundred dollars," Bianca supplied.

Madison's eyes widened. "It would take a lot for me to spend that kind of money on what's really nothing more than a glorified sex toy."

"Ah," Izzy reiterated, "but what a way to go broke."

"There's two opposing options for marketing this product," Bianca continued. "We either pitch it to women as a sexy nightie that enhances foreplay, or just go with the nickname that's already out there and admit that, yeah, it's a modern-day chastity belt and market it to guys. If you want to keep tabs on your woman, buy this lingerie and you'll sleep better knowing that she's not sleeping around."

"Do they make a male version of this?" Emma asked. "'Cause I sure would have loved to strap one on Ryan. Then it might not have been such a shock when he suddenly told me he was getting married. Now *that* product, I'd pay for."

Bianca shook her head. "No male version yet. But maybe I'll bring that up to *Senhor* Santos when I see him."

"You know what would make me buy it in a heartbeat?" Izzy mused.

Something in her voice caught Bianca's attention. Something told her for once, Izzy was being serious. Bianca sat up straighter and studied her friend. Izzy had a wealth of sexual experience. On this particular topic, her opinion was the most valuable. "What?"

"If I had some assurance that it could really work as a chastity belt."

Bianca, Madison and Emma stared at her with dropped jaws.

"What?" Izzy frowned. "Why are you all staring at me?"

"You? Not wanting to have sex?" Emma said. "Since when?"

"When it lands me into trouble like last summer. How was I to know Jackson was married to a congresswoman?"

"Um, you could have had a long conversation with him before popping into bed," Madison pointed out.

Izzy snapped her fingers. "Exactly. When I get aroused there's no stopping me. It's as if hormones switch off my brain and caution flies right out the window."

"It doesn't when you're around Hunter," Madison said, mentioning Izzy's next-door neighbor.

"Oh, it does." Izzy nodded. "Believe me, when I see that man working out at the gym, whew." She licked her lips.

"So why not go for it? Hunter is a great guy."

"Because we've been friends for so long, I can't risk spoiling it. Besides, he's got a girlfriend." She sighed. "It's always been that way with us. When I have a boyfriend, he's free and when I'm free, he's got a girlfriend. I think it's the universe's way of telling us we're better off friends."

"That's a shame."

"If that thing—" she pointed at the lingerie Emma was now investigating "—could help me get control of my impulses, I'd happily shell out two hundred for it."

"You mean if you had someone to monitor you while you're wearing it, like, maybe one of us." Bianca toggled a finger from Emma to Madison to herself, "and when we detected that your vital signs were going up, we'd just give you a call and tell you to cool it."

"Yes, and even if I turned it off you could call and talk some sense into me. You know," Izzy said, "sort of like an intervention."

"Isn't that a bit intimate?" Madison asked.

"Hey, as highly sexed as I am, I need all the help I can get," Izzy exclaimed.

"So you really *would* use it as a chastity belt, and not a sex toy?" Bianca questioned.

"Well, you know me…" Izzy shrugged.

"The world is your sex toy," Emma finished for her.

"After the disastrous romances we all had last summer," Bianca mused, "Izzy's idea doesn't sound so farfetched."

The previous year Bianca thought she'd found the perfect guy. Richard had been everything she believed she wanted in a man, an eager, competitive, responsible, goal-oriented overachiever just like her. They'd hit it off during a game of water volleyball at an all-inclusive resort in Jamaica. Bianca had been there on a corporate retreat. Richard had claimed he was scouting out investment opportunities. He seduced her with banana daiquiris and long, wet, hot kisses.

One thing led to another and Bianca ended up spilling more than just a little pillow talk. She'd wakened with one helluva hangover and discovered too late that Richard had actually been working for a competing ad agency. He'd stolen her ideas and presented them as his own to the clients she'd been courting. This was the Big Mistake she'd been cautioned against repeating.

The memory still stung. She'd received a strict reprimand from her boss and it had taken her the better part of the year to crawl out of the doghouse. She hadn't dated since. The truth was she no longer trusted herself around the opposite sex. She'd allowed her hormones to rule her head, something she sorely regretted and had never done before or since. This new client was her opportunity to make amends and fast track her career.

"As if this underwear could stop Izzy from doing whatever she had it in her mind to do," Madison said.

"I can just imagine how that conversation would go," Emma threw in. "We call Izzy at one in the morning, ordering her to put her panties back on and go home. She's just going to tell us exactly where we can stick those panties."

"Hey!" Izzy grumbled.

Bianca smiled at her. "You know it's true, Izz. We love you, but you've got a mind of your own and you've never let anyone stop you from using it."

"You are a passionate woman." Emma nodded.

"Celibacy just isn't in your nature," Madison added.

"So that's how it is. And you call yourselves my friends." Izzy folded her arms over her chest and looked affronted, but they knew she was teasing. Not much fazed Izzy.

"Only your true friends will give it to you straight." Bianca took the lingerie from Emma, folded it up and nestled it back inside the box.

Izzy sank her hands on her hips. "So you're saying I can't go without sex, but the three of you can?"

"Pretty much." Bianca grinned and tucked the box underneath her chair.

"Yes," Madison remarked bluntly.

"Um…well…" Emma hedged.

"I dare you to put your money where your mouth is," Izzy challenged.

"What do you mean?" Bianca settled her hands in her lap.

"I'm proposing a bet."

"What kind of bet?" Emma asked.

Izzy notched her chin in the air. "I bet I can go without sex longer than any of you can."

Bianca tried not to smile, but lost the battle.

Madison snickered.

"You're serious?" Emma laughed.

"As a heart attack. Five hundred dollars apiece, no sex of any kind for an entire month. Winner take all," Izzy dared.

"By 'no sex of any kind'—" Bianca started to ask.

"No oral sex, no hand jobs, and no self pleasuring," Izzy laid down the ground rules.

"Hard core." Madison made a face.

"Yes, well, I'm tired of being the laughingstock."

"We weren't laughing at you," Bianca tried to smooth things over.

"But you find the idea of me winning a celibacy contest hilarious."

"In our defense," Emma countered, "you do have a lot of sex, Izzy."

"Maybe this talk about chastity has made me realize I require some perspective about men and relationships. If celibacy can give me a clear head, then I'm willing to give it a shot."

"Did something else happen?" Bianca asked. "Do you want to spill?"

Izzy made a face. "Never mind about that."

"You don't need to be ashamed of your sexuality," Emma said.

"I'm not ashamed, I'm just thinking maybe I should step back and reevaluate things. So who's in?"

Madison raised a hand. "This one is in the bag and I could use the money. I'm going to be in Costa Rica for the entire month with a bunch of botanists searching the jungle for rare orchids. No chance for romance there."

"Hey, count me in," Emma said. "After Ryan, swearing off men for a month sounds just fine with me."

"B?" Izzy shot a glance at Bianca.

"I'm Miss Workaholic. When would I have time for romance?" Bianca asked.

"I don't know," Izzy said in a sing-songy voice. "Thomaz Santos did design that Catch Me if You Can underwear. He sounds *muito macho* to me."

"Phhttt, he's a client, no way am I falling for him." Bianca waved a hand.

"So you're in?" Izzy's grin sharpened.

"I'm in."

"And you're not the least bit worried about *Senhor* Santos?"

"Why should I worry? You'll be out in twenty-four hours," Bianca predicted.

Izzy rubbed her palms together. "We shall see."

"So how's it going to work?" Madison asked. "How are we going to keep this thing honest?"

"Can you get your hands on three more of those things?" Izzy asked Bianca.

Bianca nodded. "That can be arranged."

"Okay, so we wear the lingerie all the time. If we have to take it off for bathing and laundry and swimming and things like that, we simply send out a text letting each other know what's going on. We set up a rotating schedule to monitor each other. We'll have everybody's access codes, so we're alerted when things are heating up. If we turn off the belt without prior approval, we're automatically disqualified."

"That's reasonable," Bianca said.

"Let's make a pact." Izzy laid her palm in the middle of the table.

Emma stacked her hand over Izzy's and Madison put her hand on Emma's and Bianca topped the pile.

"All month, no sex, may the strongest woman win."

NIGHT WHISPERS

1

All work and no play makes Bianca a dull girl...or does it?

"FROM A marketing standpoint," Bianca began, shifting uncomfortably on the plush chaise lounge.

Whenever she moved she felt the silky material of the Catch Me if You Can lingerie glide across her skin like warm water. The sensation was wholly erotic and quite frankly, unsettling. Over the ephemeral garment, she wore a gray, knee-length pencil skirt and a buttoned-up white cotton blouse with sensible gray pumps and pearls. Her hair was swept up in a sleek French twist, giving her what she hoped was an air of up-and-coming young executive on the go. "You have to decide if you're selling celibacy or sex."

She still couldn't believe she was here. Bianca St. James—the woman who in high school was voted most likely to end up CEO of her own company, the woman who had written a mission statement for her life when she was a

college freshman, the woman who'd spent the ensuing nine
years throwing herself full tilt into her career—was sitting
poolside with a near-naked man, a potent umbrella drink
getting sweaty in her hand, at two o'clock on a Tuesday
afternoon in Rio de Janeiro.

It was a scenario for disaster and, after the previous
summer, Bianca had learned her lesson. No summer fun
in the sun while she was working—although technically
it was winter in Brazil.

They were on the penthouse rooftop of a downtown
Rio office building that overlooked the Atlantic Ocean.
The place was straight out of *Condé Nast Traveler.* Sleek
and ultra-modern in design, the stark-white open-air inte-
riors possessed clean, smooth lines, while at the same time
overtly whispering money, money, money. The roof was
no different. Behind them stood a blue-and-white-striped
cabana. A bowl of exotic fruits lay on the table between
them. The ocean breeze caressed her skin and scattered
the scent of the city over them—coffee beans and coconut
oil and sea foam and sugar cane.

The pool was a long rectangle, the turquoise water coolly
inviting on the warm June day. White chaise longues with
cushions to match the water were strategically positioned
on the exotic white stone of the pool area. Numerous large
potted palms in decorative clay pots added a bit of greenery. A beautiful, dark-haired woman in a pink string bikini
manned the mahogany bar a few feet away. The white marble wall behind her was mirrored, reflecting back at them
the gleaming array of liquors in their colorful bottles—
golden whiskey, pink vodka, blue curaçao, deep-brown
rum.

The swarthy man beside Bianca wore nothing more
than a pair of darkly tinted sunglasses and swim trunks in

a stunning color of azure that matched the peaceful sky overhead and accentuated his darkly tanned skin.

Although she'd met *Senhor* Santos several times before, it had always been in the buttoned-up offices of Stillman, Burke and Hollister, and Thomaz had been dressed in sleek Italian tailor-made suits that perfectly fitted his large muscular frame.

And she'd never been alone with him.

All traces of the civilized executive she thought she knew had disappeared, leaving nothing but pure, primal man. Here was the earthy playboy she'd heard so much about.

She'd never seen a face quite like this one. His angular cheekbones carved in sharp lines, he was dangerously handsome without a hint of softness. His hair was darker than an underground cavern and his body…oh, damn his body…she'd been avoiding looking at it ever since she'd taken the seat next to him. Trepidation bit at her with sharp teeth.

"In essence, Mr. Santos, you can't row your boat in two directions at once," Bianca went on, wondering if his eyes were open or closed on the other side of those expensive designer sunglasses.

She'd been here for a good five minutes and he hadn't once budged from his lounging position, or given so much as a hint that he was even aware she was sitting beside her. But she refused to let it show that he unnerved her.

"I cannot speak of business while you are so uncomfortable," Thomaz Santos said.

"I'm not uncomfortable," Bianca denied.

She crossed her legs and pressed her knees together tightly. The provocative lingerie moved with her, rubbing gently against her bottom. She'd never in her life been so aware of an undergarment and it threw her off-kilter. What was the thing made of? It felt sensual, luxurious. Better question, why had she agreed to Izzy's silly bet in the first place?

"Please, *bonita,* you are fooling no one but yourself. There is perspiration on your upper lip and you sit as if you have a steel rod thrust up your spine. Relax. Go pick out a swimsuit for yourself." He waved at the rack of skimpy swimsuits parked nearby. She assumed it was inventory from his business. "Cool off in the pool."

Bonita.

He'd just called her beautiful. It both pleased her and irritated her. "Mr. Santos," she said waspishly, "let's get something straight right up front."

He smiled wryly. "And what is that?"

"In my country calling me beautiful at a business meeting could be construed as sexual harassment." Not that this encounter was remotely like a business meeting. Dammit, she wished he'd take off those sunglasses so she could read what was going on in his eyes.

His smile deepened. "Ah, but thankfully we are not in your country. We are in Brazil and thus I am free to tell a beautiful woman that she is beautiful without threat of legal action."

"Please don't do that. I find it unsettling."

"Then you are an oddity." He shook his head as if he couldn't believe such a thing existed. "A woman who does not like to hear she is beautiful."

That made her feel all tingly. She should not be feeling tingly. She did not like feeling tingly. "Business is business, attractiveness should not enter into it."

Then he laughed as if she was the most amusing thing he'd encountered all week. "Attractiveness always enters into it."

For the first time since she'd entered his hedonistic

domain, Thomaz sat up, swinging his tanned, muscular, polo-playing legs over the side of the chaise. She dropped her gaze, noticed how he sat casually, his austerely beautiful arms draped on his thighs, his big hands resting between his open knees.

He raised his designer sunglasses onto his forehead, revealing lustrous ebony eyes fringed with dark, heavy lashes. He cast a long, lingering glance over her body.

Bianca swallowed and nervously touched the tip of her tongue to the apex of her upper lip.

Do not look at his chest.

But her eyes had minds of their own and slowly took in from his face to his finely muscled chest and granite-solid stomach. Except for the slight fabric of his swim trunks, Thomaz was practically nude. She could almost feel the velvet of his flesh, the warmth and steel beneath. Could almost taste the tangy salt of his skin. Vitality vibrated off him, projecting like heat rays off the sun.

Her entire body broke out in a sweat and she was inflamed. *It's just the sun,* she told herself, but she knew that was a bald-faced lie.

From the bar came the sound of samba music, a steady, seductive beat. Someone had switched on the satellite radio. Bianca's hips itched to sway in time to the drumming, but she primly resisted the urge.

"I am going for a swim," he said. "You'll have to join me if you want to continue discussing business. You can select a swimsuit and change in the cabana."

Thomaz levered himself off the chaise and with the elegant stroll of a man accustomed to getting what he wanted, he sauntered down the steps of the pool.

He dove into the pool, swam for a minute, and then surfaced, treading water. His dark hair was plastered against his skull. "Come in, the water is fine."

Bianca hesitated, perched on the edge of her chaise. She didn't want to go swimming with him, but it appeared to be the only option if she was hoping to get any business done today. Reluctantly, she went over to the rack of colorful swimsuits and browsed through them. Ninety percent were far too skimpy—string bikinis and thongs and even pubikinis, heaven forbid. She hadn't waxed extensively enough for any of these contenders and besides, she'd never been a two-piece kind of gal. Didn't anyone in Brazil wear a one-piece? Okay, here was a slingshot, but that was still a bikini.

After much digging, she finally found a keyhole one-piece in vivid scarlet and brash orange. Not something she would have chosen. Bianca only swam for exercise and preferred a sensible maillot in a dark color, but this suit was the best she could do under the circumstances.

With her purse slung over her shoulder and the flimsy material in her hand, she stepped into the cabana to change, but just as she unzipped her skirt, she realized she was going to have to do something about the chastity belt. Fishing her phone from her purse, she simultaneously shimmied out of her skirt. She texted her friends with her thumb while she kicked off her pumps.

Going swimming. Expect to be turned off for thirty minutes. Cheers, B.

That ought to give her enough time to get this over with and get back into her clothes.

She finished undressing and put on the swimsuit. The keyhole was cut out right at her navel. Good thing she did her sit-ups regularly. Otherwise this thing would definitely not be happening.

"Here goes nothing," she muttered and wrapped a fluffy white beach towel around her waist.

Bianca stepped outside the cabana and noticed someone—most probably the bartender—had moved their drinks poolside. She walked to the water's edge and dropped the towel on the cement beside the steps just before she got in.

"Ah." Thomaz gave her a knowing glance. "The keyhole. I am not surprised."

Irritation nudged her again. "What does that mean?"

"It's the most modest suit in that particular collection," he said.

"What is it? The Flaming Harlot collection?"

Thomaz laughed and moved closer. She was standing in five feet of water and found herself retreating up to the edge.

Bianca cleared her throat. Ridiculous, letting him get her on the run. She was taking command of the situation. "So, back to your ad campaign. You have to make a decision. Choose celibacy and market the garment as a modern-day chastity belt to men, or choose sex and market it to women as a bedroom toy."

His gaze flicked down the length of her legs, the smile on his lips smug. "We cannot do both?"

She shook her head. "It doesn't work that way. You need a focus."

His eyes were on hers now, cradling her in sharply focused study.

Bianca straightened her shoulders, trying to look totally capable and professional—very difficult to do in a keyhole swimsuit in a high-end swimming pool atop a penthouse. She wasn't about to let this man know how much his sexy masculinity unnerved her. So she stopped moving, stayed very still and stared calmly back at him. In his eyes she spied an amalgamation of amusement, brashness and desire. Her pulse pushed restlessly through her veins, but she managed to drag her gaze away from him.

"Have you tried out my product?" he asked in a husky voice.

"Um…I have." She decided not to tell him she'd worn his lingerie to the meeting.

"And what do you think?"

"It's…um…interesting."

A smirk danced at the corners of his wide mouth. "Damning with faint praise. So what is it for you? Chastity belt or a sex toy?"

"It's a business assignment, nothing more."

He shook his head and clicked his tongue. "There you go again, looking at the world from inside the confines of your box."

That made her mad.

"You know nothing about me. I've won awards for my out-of-the-box thinking. I'm an out-of-the-box-thinking creative wonder." She huffed.

"I'm *trying* to get to know you," he said mildly. "In a relaxed environment. Which is why I have a proposal for you."

He called this relaxing? Maybe to him. To her, it was like toeing a high wire stretched across the Grand Canyon. "What is that?"

"We work by day, but by night you spend your time with me relaxing."

Oh, no way, no how, dude. Shades of Richard all over again. "Relaxing isn't my style," she said curtly. "I work better under pressure."

"How can you be so sure? Have you ever tried working when you are relaxed?"

Uh, no, no, she hadn't. "This argument is going in circles."

"So, you too notice how ridiculous it is for you to argue with me." He swam even closer, invading her personal space.

He was making her lose her cool in a way no one ever had. He was handsome and charming and accustomed to getting his way—a wealthy playboy who expected women to fall at his feet. Well, he was in for a rude awakening if that's what he expected from her. To hide her nervousness, she reached for her drink positioned at the edge of the pool and feigned a sip.

"Is your drink not to your liking?"

"Huh?" She blinked, her thoughts fuzzy-edged and murky.

"Your glass is still full. I could have Maria make you another." He gestured toward the pink-bikinied barmaid who was wiping down the glistening chrome-and-glass bar with a white terrycloth towel.

"My drink is fine, I'm simply not accustomed to consuming alcohol so early in the day or during the week."

"You don't enjoy life until the weekend evenings?" He made a noise of disapproval.

"I work a lot."

"I can tell," he said, still with the disapproving tone.

"Where I come from, working a lot is considered an admirable thing."

"No wonder my lingerie is not selling well in your country. Your people have no time for pleasure and play."

"There's more to life than just having a good time," she snapped.

"How would you know?" he asked, "since by your own admission you do not make time to enjoy yourself."

"I enjoy my job. That's how I enjoy myself."

"Are you sure, *bonita?* Perhaps you work because you

are lonely and doing tasks helps fill the empty space inside you." He fisted his right hand and used it to tap twice over his heart, the water rippling with his movements.

She wished he'd stop calling her beautiful. It was distracting. "We're getting off track here. I came to Rio to help you find a way to market your product in America."

"We are not off track. We are precisely on track. You cannot market me or my product until you understand me."

Bianca blew out her breath. She could feel the account— and her potential promotion—slipping through her fingers. "What are you saying?" she muttered in his native language.

"You may be able to speak Portuguese," he said, "but you do not possess a Brazilian soul."

Bianca scowled. "Of course not, I'm American."

"But your eyes, your hair, your features, they speak of your Brazilian heritage that apparently you aren't very familiar with. It is a shame."

He was right about that. Her mother had taught her Portuguese and the samba, but Bianca's mom had come to America from Brazil when she was only eight years old and she'd quickly adapted, letting go of her old life in order to embrace the new one. She didn't live in the past, but looked always toward the future.

"As I said, you cannot help me, *bonita*, until you understand me." Thomaz's eyes glittered seductively in the sunlight. "My culture, my world."

"That doesn't make any sense. I'm here to sell you to an American audience. I should be the one teaching you about American culture."

He studied her a long moment. "Perhaps you have a point."

Whew. At last he seemed to be listening. It took all

the willpower she had not to climb from the pool and run away.

"So," Thomaz said. "Back to my proposal. You are scheduled to be in Brazil for ten days, no?"

"That is correct."

He cocked his head, came up with another devil-may-care grin. "We spend the nights doing things my way. You learn to relax and learn the Brazilian way of life, and then we spend the days with you schooling me in how American commerce works. Otherwise..." He spread his arms and shrugged, his implication clear. Either do what he wanted or he'd take his business elsewhere.

"I really don't see the point," Bianca protested.

"Then you do not agree?"

She wanted to say, *Hell no, I don't agree and I'm not going to let you manipulate me into playing games.* But then she imagined having to call her boss and explain how she'd blown the account. "That's not what I said."

"Then we have a meeting of the minds."

"We have a meeting of the minds," she said grudgingly.

"We must celebrate with a toast." He reached over to pick up his tumbler from the edge of the pool and raised his glass. It contained the same clear liquid infused with slices of lime that was in her drink. A *caipirinha*, he'd told her it was called. "To a successful merger between Brazil and America."

"To America and Brazil," she echoed, clinked the lip of her glass to his and then took a sip of the sweet, potent beverage.

As the liquid burned an icy path on the way down her throat and Thomaz Santos held her pinned with his wolfish gaze, a startling thought occurred to Bianca.

Had she just struck a bargain with the devil?

THOMAZ studied Bianca through half-lidded eyes. The brilliant red of her swimsuit accentuated the gorgeous color of her light-brown skin. He couldn't stop himself from staring. He'd never seen a woman so in need of good, honest lovemaking. Not just hard-driving sex, either—although the prim, tight way she held herself told him she needed that, too—but this woman was desperate for both tenderness and long, lingering foreplay to teach her exactly what physical delights her body was capable of experiencing.

And he'd wanted to be her teacher since he'd first laid eyes on her two months earlier in the lobby of Stillman, Burke and Hollister. Something about her compelled Thomaz in a way he could not explain. It was more than just her beauty. Brazil was chock-full of beautiful women, and with his money and charm he had no problem getting any woman he wanted. But the distrustful look in her eyes and the stubborn set to her chin told him Bianca was not like other women.

Immediately, he'd been intrigued. This one was different. This one had not only brains and beauty, but moxie to spare. And beneath it all was a hint of old-fashioned shyness. Bianca St. James was the whole package, and he knew at once that his mother would have loved her.

You need a woman with a strong will, Thomaz. Why do you date these vapid Barbie dolls with no substance? she'd asked him on more than one occasion.

"Listen to your mother," his father would say affectionately and sling his arm over his wife's shoulder. "She's always right."

His mom would nudge Poppy in the ribs, they would laugh and kiss each other. They were both gone now; the smiling mother with soft hands and the hushed fragrance of nutmeg, the doting father with a thick moustache and teasing eyes.

How he still missed them.

Idly, Thomaz wondered what his parents would think of him now. Of what he'd done with his grandmother's business. How he'd expanded her legacy. Of that, they would be proud. But of his personal life? No doubt they'd be disappointed. Wondering why at thirty-two he hadn't married and produced a passel of children.

In truth? He'd never found any relationship that could come close to what his mother and father had shared. The playboy lifestyle suited him and for the most part, he was happy. He enjoyed the company of women. Tall ones, short ones, thin ones, curvy ones, blondes, brunettes, redheads. He had no preference. He loved their soft skin and long legs and the illogical way their minds worked, so different from men and yet so disarming.

His gaze flicked over Bianca and he felt a strange pull he'd never quite experienced before. *This one,* the purling breeze seemed to whisper. *She's the one.*

That thought unsettled him and he wondered where in the hell it had come from. It was irrational. He'd never thought such a thing before, and yet there it was, circling his brain like a prayer.

Bianca took a long pull on the straw in her drink. He kept watching her, savoring the way her eyes widened and her tongue flicked out to lick away the drop of *caipirinha* that had fallen onto her bottom lip.

"There's just one issue I want to get straight," Bianca spoke but he could barely hear her, he was so busy staring at her sweet pink mouth.

"Mmm," he murmured, wishing he could pull her up against him for a hungry taste.

"Our relationship is strictly professional."

"But of course," he said, "what made you think otherwise?"

She looked caught off-guard by his question, but then recovered quickly. "Your reputation precedes you."

"Ah," he murmured, coming so near that they were almost touching. "That." He playfully cast a glance over his shoulder as if searching for eavesdroppers and lowered his voice to a teasing croon. Twin spots of pink flushed her cheeks. "What have you heard?"

"I…um…uh…" she stammered. "You know."

Thomaz liked the way her eyes widened and her lips tightened when she got flustered, but he could tell she was struggling hard not to show that he'd knocked her off balance. "How could I know if the talk is going on behind my back?"

She swept a hand at the penthouse rooftop. "You're a man who appreciates his indulgences."

"Any specifics on what those indulgences are?" he teased.

"Drinks in the middle of the day…" She held up her glass.

"And?"

She cleared her throat. "Umm… It's rumored you're a flirt and something of a dynamo in the sack."

"Sack?" Thomaz didn't quite understand the English idiom.

"It's slang for bed."

Intriguing. "So I'm good in bed," he restated. He arched an eyebrow and grinned.

Bianca shrugged. "That's the rumor."

"Where did you hear it?"

"Actually, in the elevator on the way up. Two women were talking about you, one said you were a wonderful kisser and the other…" The color on Bianca's cheeks darkened and she ducked her head, crossed her arms over her chest. "She said kissing wasn't even your best bedroom skill."

"Did she elaborate?"

Bianca squirmed. "Um...the word *tantric* might have been mentioned."

"Ah."

"And...um..." She was speaking so softly he could barely understand her. "Something about an hour-long orgasm."

He could tell she was wondering if such a thing was even possible. "I'm a man who takes his time."

Bianca gulped visibly. "Anyway, I'm trying to be clear that I'm not going to have sex with you, tantric or otherwise."

She was lying about that. The pulse jumping at the hollow of her throat gave her away.

"Just because I know how to enjoy myself doesn't mean I'm interested in you, either." No way was he confessing the truth; that in his mind he was already making love to her.

"You're not?"

"You're a beautiful woman, Ms. St. James, but I am not interested in anyone who is not interested in me."

She blew out her breath. "Oh. Well then, that's great."

"It does make me wonder, however, what you're so afraid of."

"Me?" She tossed her head and Thomaz had a wild desire to take the pins from her hair and watch the sable strands cascade to her shoulders. There was that blush again, bringing high color to her cheeks, and suddenly Thomaz just *knew* that this woman had never had an orgasm. At least not with a lover.

"I'm not afraid of anything."

He couldn't resist teasing her. "Not even one-hour orgasms?"

2

PROMPTLY at 8:00 p.m., Bianca opened the door to Thomaz's knock.

He stepped over the threshold smelling provocatively of leather and sunshine, and raked his gaze over her. A smile tipped his lips. "You look very beautiful."

Bianca raised an index finger. "No compliments. That's crossing the line. This is a business arrangement and nothing more."

He nodded, but somehow the expression on his face seemed to say, *that's what you think.*

She was being fanciful and probably reading way more into it than he ever intended. Feeling flustered, Bianca glanced around the room for her purse and spied it on the end of the bed. She scooped it up and raised her head to see Thomaz's eyes on the bed. Was he thinking what she was thinking? What the hell *was* she thinking?

One-hour orgasms.

Electricity fairly crackled in the air between them. Thomaz extended his arm. "Shall we?"

She took his elbow even though it wasn't smart, but she couldn't fight him on everything. It was exhausting, constantly being on guard. He escorted her downstairs, tossed the valet his keys. She let go of his elbow while they waited for the valet to bring the car around.

She wasn't surprised when a low-slung, red Ferrari convertible pulled up in front of them and the valet got out. Perfect car for a playboy. Thomaz tipped him an obscene amount of money and then opened the passenger door for Bianca. The back of her arm brushed against his shoulder as she climbed in and instantly hot sparks of awareness shot through her.

This was going to be a long ten days.

Think of something else. Business. That always works. She narrowed her eyes, collected her thoughts. *Business. Yes.*

Why was her mind suddenly blank? Did it have something to do with the man sliding behind the wheel, gripping the gearshift with his strong, broad fingers?

Determinedly, she glanced out the window as he put the Ferrari in gear and zoomed off. The lively streets were crowded with people. The air smelled of the tropics, rich and floral and fruity.

Thomaz came to a stop outside a valet stand in front of an elegant restaurant built with white stone and decorated with black wrought-iron fencing. The parking lot was packed, and delicious smells wafted in the air—roasted meats, exotic spices, sizzling onions and garlic. Bianca's mouth watered. Thomaz claimed her arm again and guided her into the restaurant. She didn't know what to think about his proprietary touch or the fact that she sort of enjoyed it.

The material of his silk suit grazed her side. Tailored, luxurious, the suit fitted him like a glove. The maître d' greeted Thomaz as if he was a long-lost brother and spared an appraising stare for Bianca. Probably assuming she was the billionaire's latest conquest.

Bianca proudly tossed her head and lifted her shoulders. She was no one's conquest.

The maître d' escorted them upstairs to a table with a stunning view of the ocean. Her heart skipped a beat at the breathtaking beauty of the water bathed in moonlight. Thomaz pulled out her chair for her and she was so near she could smell his cologne—a bracing fragrance, hearty and substantial. Not what she would have expected from a playboy billionaire. She sat and he retreated to take his own chair. The maître d' unfurled the linen napkin onto her lap. Discreet, top-notch service. She wondered how many women Thomaz brought here. Hundreds probably.

The sommelier hurried over and without even asking her preference, Thomaz ordered a bottle of very expensive white wine.

"Don't feel you have to spend a lot of money to impress me," Bianca said. "I'm not impressed by wastefulness."

Thomaz chuckled. "I would ask for the same whether you were with me or I was alone, *bonita,* no need to get your back up."

Was she being overly sensitive? Probably. She could so easily see herself getting swept away with his bold, grand gestures—the city, the fast car, the elegant restaurant, the overpriced wine. All the stuff of a glorious seduction. Well, he'd picked the wrong woman to wow. She refused to be seduced.

The sommelier returned and went through the ritual of uncorking the bottle and giving Thomaz a taste for his approval. Thomaz nodded and the wine steward poured two glasses.

The waiter came over and again Thomaz ordered for them both. As an independent woman, Bianca chafed at his take-charge manner, but a secret part of her thrilled at his polished command and she had to admit it was nice not always having to be in control.

"You do eat meat?" Thomaz asked after the waiter disappeared.

In that instant of hesitation, she saw vulnerability slip across his face. The man wasn't quite as self-assured as he wanted everyone to believe.

"Yes."

He smiled and looped his arm around the back of his chair in a cocky slouch, his uncertainty vanishing so quickly she wondered if she'd imagined it. And there was definitely no uncertainty in the way he was looking at her now.

Her womb jumped with a swift squeeze of ravenous need, a deep-seated tightening of desire. A sizzling hot wetness slicked her body. She had to calm down, get hold of herself or one of her friends would soon be ringing her cell phone and asking if she was losing her head to temptation. Bianca drew in a slow, deep breath.

"You seem more relaxed already," he said.

"I'm feeling more relaxed." The deep breathing worked wonders.

This time his smile was unexpectedly gentle and Bianca felt something unspool inside her.

"Thomaz! I thought that was you." A man's voice broke the silence.

Thomaz's smile changed from intimate to public as he raised his head to greet the round-faced man about his own age walking up to their table.

"Philippe." He stood and they clasped each other in a hearty embrace.

Philippe cast a glance at Bianca and she saw surprise cross his face. What was that all about?

"I was having dinner with some clients and saw you

over here. I had to come by and say thank you, thank you, a million times thank you." Philippe said in Portuguese and pumped Thomaz's hand.

He was talking fast but Bianca could understand the gist of the conversation.

"You have brought my wife and I much joy, much happiness." He turned to Bianca. "You are with a very great man."

She halfway expected the guy to genuflect.

Thomaz looked embarrassed and Bianca could have sworn he was blushing beneath his deep tan. "It was not me, Philippe—"

"You are too modest." Philippe's face was animated and Bianca could tell he meant every word. "Not many rich men give of themselves and their money so generously."

Thomaz squirmed under Philippe's praise. "I'm glad I could help your family. Give them my best, would you?"

"I will." Philippe beamed. "Well, I won't keep you from your dinner." He waved and walked back to his table.

Bianca studied Thomaz in the flickering candlelight. "What was that all about?"

"It was nothing." But his voice went soft, the expression in his eyes even softer.

It was the first time she'd seen him so… She couldn't find the right word. *Peaceful* was close, but it was more than that. With a sense of purpose maybe?

Curiosity fluttered inside her. The man was much more complex than she'd guessed. His good deed—whatever it was—and the fact he was uncomfortable acknowledging it, raised her respect and cancelled out some of the wild rumors she'd heard about him. Thomaz Santos grew more intriguing by the minute.

The waiter brought their food. Thomaz had ordered several dishes so they could share. Appetizers of *enroladinhos* filled with shrimp, crabmeat and a spicy sauce on the side. The entrées included *picadinho*—a diced beef traditionally served with rice, beans, baby banana and a poached egg—*salmão com molho de açaí*—wild salmon filet with açai sauce served over yucca puree and julienne vegetables, and *espeto de linguiça*—lamb-and-spicy-sausage skewers served with roasted potato, onion and sweet peppers.

"So what else is there to know about Thomaz Santos that I might never have guessed?" she asked over the delicious meal.

"I'm a simple man." He tried to look humble. It had the same effect as an elephant trying to hide behind a sapling.

She laughed. "You are anything but simple, Thomaz Santos."

He reached across the table and laid his hand over hers. His touch sent her pulse skyrocketing and she had to take in another long, slow, deep breath to get herself under control. Being around this man was as unpredictable as a roller-coaster ride. Full of rising heights and sharp curves and sudden plunges. Part of her couldn't wait to see what would happen next, another part of her wanted to flee while she could still get out unscathed.

"Let's not talk about me," he said. "I am boring as laundry. Tell me about Bianca St. James. How does a woman who speaks such beautiful Portuguese acquire a last name like St. James?"

"My father," she said. "His family were missionaries to South America when he was young. For a time they worked here in the slums of Rio and an eight-year-old orphan girl touched their hearts and his family adopted her. The girl was my mother. As they grew older, she and my father fell in love. Mom put Brazil behind her, but she did teach me and my brothers and sister how to speak Portuguese."

His eyes darkened and his face softened. He squeezed her hand, still resting underneath his. "Your mother sounds like a unique woman."

"She's strong and dedicated. She and Dad spent their whole lives building their pizza business in Brooklyn. I grew up waiting tables and hand-tossing pizza dough and reading bedtime stories to my siblings."

"You're the oldest."

She nodded.

"That explains the work ethic."

"What's wrong with having a strong work ethic?'

"Nothing is wrong with it."

"But you say it like it it's a bad thing."

"Not a bad thing, *bonita,* but it shouldn't be the *only* thing. Life is a buffet, but you're still just eating pizza."

"Nice analogy."

"Sarcasm?"

"How could you tell?"

"I know you, it feels as if I've always known you," he said looking deeply into her eyes.

That comment completely took the wind from her sails. Even as she felt the frisson of pleasure swim through her, Bianca knew it was stupid to fall under this playboy's charming spell. He probably said the same thing to every woman he dated.

"So what made you go into advertising? Why not food service?" he asked.

Bianca shrugged. "When I was a kid my parents really struggled with the restaurant. Then, one of their friends convinced them to advertise. They were nervous about spending the money, but they took the leap and it resulted in a big jump in their business. I saw firsthand how advertising could really make a difference. Especially to small-business owners like my parents. Plus, my brother Joey decided against college to help my folks run the business and Joey and I tend to butt heads. The pizza business just isn't big enough for the two of us."

"And yet you are working for a large firm and handling big accounts like mine."

"As nice as it is to help out the mom-and-pop stores, it's big business that pays the bills."

"You say that with sadness."

"I hate losing touch with my roots," she said, realizing that her job did at times feel bittersweet. She'd been hoping her promotion would help cure those counterproductive emotions.

Thomaz leaned back against his chair still cradling her hand, cocked his head and assessed her with a long, appraising glance. "You have already lost touch with your Brazilian roots."

"I know," she said. "It's one of the perks of working on this campaign. It'll give me the chance to learn about my mother's culture."

"And yet when I proposed the idea, you fought me on it."

"It wasn't learning about my mother's culture that had me dragging my feet," she admitted.

"No?"

She shook her head. She glanced down at his hand on hers, noticed his buffed, blunt-trimmed fingernails.

"Then why?"

"You. You're the reason I didn't want to agree."

"I unsettled you?"

Her heart knocked. *You have no idea.* "I just don't want to get to know you on a personal level."

"And why is that?"

"Your reputation."

"As an esteemed lover?"

"Oh, now you're just fishing for compliments."

He grinned. "Perhaps."

Another silence fell.

"I have dated many women in my life but you are different," he said pensively, as if she totally perplexed him.

"How am I different?"

"For one thing…" The grin widened. "You are not impressed with me."

"So you only like me because I don't like you?"

"You like me," he said cockily.

"I don't like your values."

"Now how can you judge me when you refuse to get to know me?"

"You do have a point," she conceded. "I'm going on what I've heard."

"See." He raised a finger. "That's why it's never a good idea to listen to gossip. If you want the truth, come to the horse's mouth."

Bianca laughed. "You're the horse's mouth? I would have thought another part of the horse's anatomy might fit."

He chuckled. "Feisty, too. I like that about you. How the outside doesn't match the inside. Outside you are buttoned-up, strict, regimented…but inside, there's a spirited woman just waiting to break out and experience all the things she's turning her nose up at."

"I don't turn my nose up."

"Perhaps you are right. Perhaps I am just as shallow as you say."

Bianca let it go and concentrated on her meal, but she couldn't stop herself from already seeing him differently. Behind that perfect smile and expensive clothes and fancy car was a man who used activity, pleasure and possessions to cover up his pain. She had a mad urge to find out what sorrow he hid from the world. To uncover the real Thomaz buried beneath the pile of money and prestige.

He took her back to the hotel after dinner and to Bianca's utter surprise he did not try to kiss her. She'd had a plan for thwarting him if he'd gone in for the smooch.

But he did nothing more than take her hand and tickle her palms with his fingers. "Goodnight, *bonita,* until tomorrow...."

3

FOR THE FIRST TIME in as long as he could remember, Thomaz left a woman's hotel without at least kissing her. He'd wanted to—more than he'd wanted to breathe—but he hadn't even tried. Any other time, with any other woman, he would have just gone in for the kiss, consequences be damned.

But Bianca was different, special. He didn't want to rush her. When she'd told him of her heritage, her family, he'd felt...intimate with her. It shook him to the core and he wasn't sure he cared for the feeling. It was thrilling, yes, but it was also very scary. For years, he'd managed to keep himself removed from other people.

You told Bianca to step outside her box; maybe you should do the same.

Both disturbed and delighted, Thomaz got into his Ferrari and headed for the highway. He drove swiftly and skillfully. In his mind he was living the James Bond fantasy, daring and suave, but in his heart, he was still the young man who'd lost his beloved parents far too soon.

He shook off the melancholy mood. This was ridiculous. He had to stop feeling sorry for himself. And he had to stop imagining that Bianca St. James was anything more than what she really was. A beautiful woman hired to help him sell lingerie. That's all she was, nothing more.

If he wasn't careful, he could fall for her and fall hard. But a man in his position couldn't afford not to be careful. There were many women out there who would love to latch onto him to get their hands on his money. Yes, she was pushing him away, but maybe she was cagier than the usual gold digger.

Seeing Philippe this evening seemed serendipitous since his old college roommate was a detective in the local police force. Considering the way he was feeling about Bianca, it might not be a bad idea to give him a call and have him do a little digging into her background.

Just to be on the safe side.

AFTER Thomaz left, Bianca tossed her purse on the desk and stripped off her clothes. She still wore the lingerie that he had invented. She stared at herself in the mirror and noticed how wild her hair looked. Strands had fallen from the ponytail, giving her a sexily disheveled appearance. She thought of Thomaz, how he'd stared at her as if she was the most gorgeous thing he'd ever seen.

Remembering caused her body to heat up. The purple and white lingerie glided silkily over her skin as she ran her arms down her waist, her imagination going berserk.

In her mind's eye, Thomaz was standing behind her. His dark head dipped as he leaned down to kiss the nape of her neck, his tongue wickedly tasting her skin. Her nipples hardened as she envisioned his fingers pinching the hardening peaks instead of her own. A soft groan slipped from her lips. Her thighs tingled and her stomach tightened.

Bianca swallowed. Erotic sensations shivered through her body. She couldn't stop thinking about him, nor could she stop touching herself. She desired him in a way she'd never wanted another. She'd heard Izzy talk of such sexual urgency, but she'd never experienced such a hunger.

No matter how hard she tried she could not stop her mind from creating delicious scenarios. Thomaz touching her in places that burned for him. Her hand crept lower from her breasts to her waist, sliding down to the edge of the skimpy little lacy panties. Her fingers were urgent as she slipped them beneath the waistband and stroked her throbbing sex. She could smell Thomaz's masculine scent. She could taste him even though she'd never kissed him.

Oh, how she'd wanted to kiss him. Her body was slick and ready, eager for entry. She slid an index finger inside her...

And that's when her cell phone rang.

Dammit.

She straightened up, ended the fantasy, snatched the cell phone from her purse and saw it was Izzy. She wanted to ignore the call and go on with her dream lover, but she knew if she did she would be out of the contest. She'd have to fork out five hundred dollars and admit she was the first one to lose the bet. Not something a driven, goal-oriented person did willingly. Sighing, she flipped open her phone. "Hello."

"Whoa, B," Izzy said. "You've got some whacked-out vital signs. Are you about to break our bet?"

"I'm all by myself," Bianca said grumpily. "There's no guy here."

"What about in your imagination?" Izzy asked.

"I'm allowed my fantasies."

"Who is it?" Izzy asked. "Your red-hot Brazilian client?"

"None of your business."

"Ooh, testy. I must have guessed correctly." Izzy chuckled.

"Is that all you wanted?"

"Just to remind you that self-pleasure, for the purpose of this bet, is considered sex. So unless you're prepared to lose, hands off the treasure."

Bianca rolled her eyes. "Seriously?"

"We all agreed."

Slowly, she let out her breath.

"So don't do it, 'kay? Although come to think of it, why am I helping you? I'm the one who badly needs the money."

"Do you need to borrow some, Izz? I've got a little saved up—"

"No way," Izzy said. "I'm winning this thing fair and square. No one thinks I can do it."

That was true. Bianca would have bet a thousand dollars that Izzy would be the first one out if she hadn't met Thomaz and learned how pathetic her self-control was. His crazy lingerie was causing all kinds of problems.

In the background, Bianca heard a man's voice. "Hey, wait a minute! You're calling me on the carpet and I hear a guy in your apartment."

"Oh, that's just Hunter. My DVR was on the fritz and he came over to tinker with it."

"That's not a euphemism for something else, is it?"

"Where do you get these ideas?"

"You."

Izzy laughed. "You have a point."

"So is anything going on with Hunter?"

"Of course not."

"Thanks for calling, Izzy. I'm sorry about being irritable."

"Hey, I understand completely. Horniness can turn the best of us into grouches."

Bianca hung up and sighed deeply. This chastity thing

was much more difficult than she'd ever imagined—
especially with a man like Thomaz Santos around.

Resolutely, she strengthened her resolve. She could resist. She only had nine more days. She'd go into his office
tomorrow morning and get right to work.

Except that it wasn't the mornings that worried her.

THOMAZ couldn't wait to get to the office the following
morning to see Bianca again. He'd dreamed of her in the
night, a red-hot sex dream that had woken him in a cold
sweat with a hard-on that wouldn't die.

And because of that dream, and his lack of willpower,
he'd called Philippe that morning and asked him to inves-
tigate Bianca.

She was already sitting in the main lobby when he arrived and sprang to her feet the minute he came through the
door. Her high heels clacked against the polished marble
as she scurried toward him.

Instantly, his body responded, his temperature on full
boil. A prickly roll of tingles started at his toes and tromped
right on up to his gut. And the hard-on he'd worked so hard
to kill at three in the morning was back, pressing irrever-
ently against his zipper.

It seemed she had grown even more beautiful overnight.
Her hair was pulled up in that lovely twist, her delicate
features utterly patrician. She wore very little makeup and
her clothes were as conservative as the business attire she'd
worn the day before, but that only seemed to enhance her
sexual allure.

Bianca's eyes met his. They were the shade of coffee
liberally laced with cream—brown and warm and inviting,
fringed with a sweep of thick lashes. He wanted to drink
from her gaze and never look away.

"It's ten minutes to ten," she remarked, "what time do your offices open anyway?"

Thomaz smiled and shook his head. "Ten o'clock, my little overachiever."

"I'm not yours," she said crossly, but her eyes softened. She was trying hard to be mad at him and failing.

"You are working for me, are you not?"

She nodded.

"Then you are mine." Yes, that sounded possessive, but she stirred the primal caveman in him that demanded he claim her as his own.

"I *work* for you. You do not own me, Thomaz Santos."

"Of course not," he deferred. "I meant no offense." He held out his arm. "Please allow me to escort you to the elevator."

He thought she wasn't going to accept the gesture, but at last, she wrapped one hand around his arm while she clutched her briefcase in the other. The minute her fingers touched him a jolt of intensity trekked up his shoulder and partied with the electric tingles that had started in his feet. Both sensations conjoined in his heart and produced a heat of pure yearning.

The hairs on the back of his neck stood up. What was this? What was happening to him? His hands yearned to rove over her body. His mouth craved to taste hers. His nose twitched, eager to smell the throbbing pulse points at her throat.

Instead he guided her from the elevator onto the top floor where his offices stretched out before them. The company headquarters were in Rio, but he had shops all over the world, employing more than 40,000 people. Santos Enterprises was his kingdom, but she was acting like the queen, her head held at a regal tilt, her posture perfect.

After a full tour of the facility, he brought her to the

conference room for a board meeting. He introduced her to the group and she took the floor. Her Portuguese wasn't perfect, but he had to give her credit for trying, and when she stumbled, she lightly poked fun at herself. She was very good at her job.

Bianca outlined her ideas for his campaign, how her company planned to create new opportunities for their products in America. The more she talked, the more animated she became. Her face glowed, her eyes danced, her breathing quickened. Clearly, she was very passionate about what she did. He felt a sense of pride at having found her, but he couldn't help wondering if that same unbridled passion would translate into the bedroom.

"We intend to make the Catch Me if You Can brand as recognizable as Victoria's Secret," she said.

That brought smiles as the twelve members of the director's board caught her enthusiasm. She dismissed the challenges facing them as if they were nothing more than landmarks she would zoom right past. By the end of the presentation, she had even the crustiest old guy on the board of directors eating from her hand.

"That seemed to go pretty well," she commented, after everyone else had left the room.

"You charmed them," he said. *You charmed me.*

How about that? The playboy tamed by the workaholic.

In that moment, Thomaz knew he'd do whatever was necessary to make her his own.

"WHERE are we going tonight?" Bianca asked, excited to be out of the office and in Thomaz's car with the top down, the wind blowing through her hair. They'd been on three more dates, each more romantic than the last. He'd taken her sailing at sunset, to an outdoor bandstand to listen and dance to love ballads under the stars, and on a picnic in the park. She wondered how he could top them tonight.

"There's something I want to show you," he said cryptically.

Intrigued, Bianca tried to guess where they might be headed. To watch the sunset? To dance the samba at a street fair? To his house? Yipes, she wasn't ready for that.

But where they ended up took her totally by surprise.

On the outskirts of Rio, Thomaz turned down a pristinely paved asphalt one-lane road surrounded by lush green fields enclosed behind white metal pole fencing where horses grazed. They drove up a circular drive to what appeared to be a mansion, and for a moment, she thought it was Thomaz's home. But then she saw the small elegant wooden sign posted on the grounds that read: Safe Haven Children's Home.

He'd brought her to an orphanage? Confused, Bianca canted her head. "What are we doing here?"

"Since your mother was once an orphan on the streets of Rio…" He stopped, suddenly looking uncertain.

"Yes?" He didn't speak for so long that she thought he wasn't going to go on. That he was going to put the Ferrari in gear and zoom away.

Finally, he said, "The plight of street children is part of Rio. I would be remiss if I showed you only the positive aspects of our culture."

The way he said *our* sent unexpected goose bumps walking up her arms. He said it as if *she* was part of Brazil.

He killed the engine and went around to help her from the passenger side. The sun was starting to fade as they walked up the cobblestone walkway to the front door. It was yanked open before they had a chance to knock and a middle-aged woman with graying hair and a happy face folded Thomaz into a big hug.

The woman chatted with him in Portuguese. Clearly the staff here knew him. Did he come to visit the orphanage often?

Then the woman glanced around Thomaz and saw Bianca standing there. She reached out a hand. "*Boa noite,* I'm Rafaella Alves."

"Bianca St. James."

Rafaella eyed her. "You are Brazilian?"

"American with Brazilian roots."

"Her mother was a street child rescued by missionaries and adopted in America," Thomaz explained.

The next thing Bianca knew, Rafaella was embracing her as though she was a long-lost daughter. "Come in, come in," she invited, ushering them inside.

The home opened up into a foyer that was both elegant and functional. They'd no sooner stepped inside than a passing child called out Thomaz's name, begging Thomaz to come play.

Thomaz's face lit up and he laughed as the boy took his hand and pulled him deeper into the massive house. Bianca hung back in the doorway, not really sure what she should do.

Rafaella stayed with her. "You must be very special to him."

Caught up in watching Thomaz with the children, Bianca started at the older woman's words. "What?"

"He's never brought anyone here before."

Why had he brought *her* here? "Does Thomaz come often?"

"At least weekly. He owns the place, you know. He built it as a legacy to his parents who were both orphans adopted to wealthy families."

That shook her to her core. A playboy who owned an orphanage? "Really?"

"He funds fifty percent of our daily expenses," Rafaella went on. "And the rest comes from donations from his wealthy friends. We wanted to name it Santos Children's Haven, but he wouldn't let us. He doesn't like people knowing he's involved."

"Why not? He should be very proud."

Rafaella shrugged. "It is a personal thing for him. It is not for praise or recognition. He simply wants to honor his parents' memory and their charity."

"Bonita," Thomaz called and motioned for her. "Come."

"Come where?"

"To play a game," the kids chorused.

"But only for a short while," Rafaella said. "Dinner is in half an hour."

Trailed by eager children, Thomaz raced across the floor to take Bianca's hand.

In the gathering dusk of twilight, Thomaz and the children dragged her to the wide expanse of rolling lawn at the back of the house. A string of colored lights stretched from the patio to the fence at the rear of the enclosure.

"What are we playing?" Bianca asked.

"Come a little closer," Thomaz murmured.

Bianca stepped closer.

Thomaz laughed. "No, that is the name of the game. Come a little closer."

He then explained the rules. It was a lot like red light, green light combined with hide-and-seek. Thomaz was to be It and a stone birdbath in the middle of the yard was base. He had to keep one part of his body on the base at all times, and from that position he could see all four quadrants of the backyard.

Thomaz closed his eyes and counted to twenty while everyone scrambled to hide. Bianca hid behind a clump of shrubbery, surprised to find her heart was thumping. She hadn't played a game like this since she was a teenager entertaining her younger siblings. Back then, she was always It and her brothers and sister got to do the hiding.

Thomaz opened his eyes and started searching for the kids. "Victor is behind the shed," he called out.

Sheepishly, Victor shrugged and went to sit on the back patio.

Thomaz said, "Come a little closer." Then he closed his eyes and counted again.

Bianca moved from the shrub to a jacaranda tree where a grinning little girl was already hiding. The child put her finger to her lips and softly giggled. "Shh."

"Marcos and Marina in the tree fort," Thomaz yelled. "Lucas behind the trellis."

Marcos, Marina and Lucas came out of hiding, but suddenly the girl beside Bianca bolted fast as a bullet toward the base.

She didn't make it. Thomaz ensnared her seconds before she touched the birdbath. "Flavia is out."

Bianca's heart was beating so loudly she could hear it in her ears.

"Come a little closer," Thomaz invited the remaining players and closed his eyes to count again.

Bianca searched for a place nearer the birdbath where she wouldn't get caught, and realized there wasn't any hideout that would camouflage her size. The kids could curl up into balls behind things, but she was too grownup for that.

"Seventeen," Thomaz called out.

Get down or he's going to see you.

Bianca didn't know what compelled her—maybe her competitive instincts—because honestly, did it really matter if he caught her or not? But she acted out of pure instinct and just dropped to the ground, splaying flat in the flower-bed, heedless of the dirt and sticks and leaves clinging to her clothes.

Thomaz opened his eyes and rattled off more names until everyone was out except Bianca. The children sat on the porch talking and laughing, the joyous sounds echoing softly.

"Bianca," he said into the darkness. "Come a little closer."

She'd have to make a run for it. Gathering her courage, she got to her feet and sprinted toward the birdbath. She reached it just as Thomaz opened his eyes. Her hand touched the cement lip just as his encircled her wrist.

"You're caught," he said huskily.

She raised her head. He smiled and Bianca could have sworn the earth moved.

"She's safe!" all the children yelled.

"Hey!" Thomaz teased. "Whose side are you on?"

"Bianca won, Bianca won!" The kids jumped up to dance around them.

Thomaz kept his gaze locked with hers, a laugh tugging at his lips. She certainly didn't feel safe.

Not in the least.

"IT IS a nice night for a stroll," Thomaz observed after dinner with Rafaella and the children. "Would you like to walk around the grounds before we head back to the city?"

"That sounds good."

Thomaz took her hand, linking his fingers through hers and Bianca didn't even try to resist.

"Why did you bring me here tonight?" she asked as they walked along the cobblestone path.

"I almost didn't."

"What made you decide to do it?"

"I guess I wanted you to know that I am more than the man who can give one-hour orgasms."

"I'm warning you," she said, "you're hyping this talent so much, you'd better be able to live up to the promise."

"Are you interested in finding out?" he teased.

Hell, yes! "I can't cross that line. You are my client. An affair could jeopardize our working relationship."

"I could hire another ad agency."

"No!"

He startled.

"I mean…don't do that, please." She didn't want to explain about Richard and the mistakes she'd made. But if he took his account away from Stillman, Burke and Hollister so he could have an affair with her, she'd lose her job for sure.

"I didn't want to do that, anyway. Your ideas intrigue me."

"Then no more talk of affairs and one-hour orgasms."

"Perhaps after the campaign is over."

"Perhaps," she said, knowing there was very little chance of that. They lived in separate countries, living completely different lifestyles.

Thomaz stopped beneath the shelter of a jacaranda tree. His eyes were hooded in the darkness, drawing her in. *"Bonita,"* he whispered.

Instinct warned her to move, but her feet were rooted to the spot. His hands closed on her shoulders and he gently drew her into his arms. She felt the hardness of his thighs pressed against hers, the crush of her breasts against the silky material of his suit jacket.

Hopelessly, she stared into his eyes, inky black pools that paralyzed her completely. Her breath escaped from her lungs and her lips parted. In spite of all the reasons why this was a bad idea, she needed to kiss him.

His hands moved up, caressing her neck, cupping the back of her head, tilting her face, his fingers splaying through her hair.

With throat-tightening languor, his mouth hovered above hers, his gaze holding her spellbound until his dark lashes closed. Swept away by the delicious heat, Bianca's eyes drifted closed, too, as his breath mingled lightly with hers.

Insects buzzed in the trees. A light breeze ruffled the leaves. She breathed in the smell of the ocean and Thomaz. And then his lips fully covered hers.

Her heart hammered at the hollow of her throat, in her ears, behind her knees. His tightening grip pressed his thighs against her hips. She burned there, blistered by the contact.

His tongue followed the outline of her lips, touching her mouth with tender pressure. Her entire body felt scorched as he pulled her up flush against him.

She opened her mouth, letting him in. He kissed as if he'd been made exclusively for it. His number-one talent.

But then there were the rumors of those one-hour orgasms. If he made love the way he kissed...*oh, my.*

Every nerve ending in her body caught fire. Her pulse raced. Her breathing swung from crazy-erratic to hardly breathing at all. Lust blinded her, hijacked her brain. She couldn't think, couldn't speak, could only kiss and kiss and kiss.

And if her cell phone hadn't rung with Emma on the other end, Bianca might have tumbled headlong into the abyss.

4
—

FOR THE remainder of the week they worked together in the office by day, and by night they went out to explore Rio. After that night at the orphanage, something had changed between them. They settled into an easy rhythm and being around him was just plain fun. Thomaz was showing her how to play and not take things so seriously. Whenever she was around him she felt freer...happier.

But there was that pesky sexual attraction. Twice more her friends had called to caution her when things had gotten heated and out of hand—once when she and Thomaz had gone to a club to dance the samba and then again when they'd gone to listen to music in an open-air café and they'd played footsie underneath the table.

After leaving the office on Friday, Thomaz announced, "Tomorrow, we're doing something special."

"We're supposed to be working," she said. "We've made big strides on your campaign and I'm leaving next Wednesday. We don't have much time left."

"And because of that we deserve a day off," he said. "I'll pick you up at seven in the morning. Dress casually and bring a change of clothing."

A change of clothing? That sounded intriguing.

The following morning, Thomaz drove her to a small airfield where his private plane awaited with his pilot to jet them to Iguaçu Falls. The day was warm and sunny.

"Did you bring a change of clothes?" Thomaz asked. "We're going to get soaking wet."

Bianca held up her beach bag. "I've been to Niagara Falls. I came prepared."

Thomaz chuckled. "Do you know what Eleanor Roosevelt said when she first saw Iguaçu Falls?"

"What's that?"

"Poor Niagara."

Bianca laughed. "Well, bring it on. I'm ready to be wowed."

The plane landed at a local airport, and from there Thomaz chartered a private boat to take just the two of them to the falls. There were definitely some perks to dating a billionaire.

You're not dating him. Don't even go there.

Maybe not, but this non-date was shaping up to be one of the best dates of her life. Iguaçu did put Niagara to shame, simply because there were so many more falls. The noise was deafening. The shower of spray cooled her heated skin. Bianca realized that Thomaz was watching her, not the water. It made her feel both self-conscious and strangely flattered.

Get over yourself. He's probably just seen the thing a million times.

Thomaz told the driver to speed up and he revved the engine to a breakneck pace that sent Bianca's blood strumming. The boat bounced over the choppy water. The cool splash of water in her face, the taste of sunshine, the thundering sounds. It all coursed through her, making her feel fresh and alive.

After the boat ride, they walked along the top of the

falls. The vistas of waterfalls and tropical jungle beyond stretched out before them, simply breathtaking. In this noisy place, Bianca felt a strange kind of peace, even as tourists thronged and helicopters dipped low over the falls.

She was so grateful Thomaz had brought her here. She turned to tell him this as they stood on a viewing platform overhanging the falls. He was leaning on the railing with his forearms a short distance from her. His hair was soaking wet and plastered rather sexily against his forehead.

He glanced over and gave her a soft grin that spread slowly across his face. All around him were rainbows, created from the sun glinting off the water spray. Thomaz Santos was glowing.

Bianca had never seen anything like it. She whipped out her camera, never mind that the lens was going to get soaked, and snapped his picture.

He reached for the camera. "My turn. I want to capture you the way you look now. Like an intoxicating water nymph."

She gave him the camera and their fingers brushed during the exchange. She felt the contact clean through to her solar plexus. The man was potent. She had to give him that. She reached up a hand to finger-comb her damp hair, but he shook his head.

"Leave it, you are beautiful."

A heated flush rose to her cheeks and she ducked her head, embarrassed by the sound of his husky voice. She turned him on. And it was completely mutual.

After the walk along the falls, they went back to the plane so they could change clothes. In the bathroom of the private jet, she'd stripped off her wet cargo pants and was about to pull on a pair of silky slacks when there was a knock on the door.

"Just a minute," she said, standing there in nothing but the chastity belt Thomaz had designed.

"I've got a glass of champagne here for you," Thomaz said, "to celebrate our first time at the falls."

He said it as if there would be many more outings and Bianca felt at once both sad and confused. She did want many more outings with Thomaz. But it was a very dangerous thing to yearn for.

She stood behind the door, opened it a crack and stuck her hand out to receive the champagne.

"You're wearing my lingerie."

"What!" How could he see her? She was behind the door and had opened it only enough for him to pass the champagne to her. Then she caught sight of herself in the mirror over the sink and realized that from his position in the hallway Thomaz could see her reflection.

She snatched the glass inside the bathroom with her and slammed the door closed. "Go away."

"You're wearing the underwear I designed." He sounded raspy, aroused.

"Of course I'm wearing your underwear," she snapped, leaning her forehead against the door. Dumb, dumb, dumb to let him get a glimpse of her with it on. "I have to get a sense of the product before I can successfully market it."

"Are you sure you're not using it against me?"

"What does that mean?"

"I have noticed whenever we're about to get to know each other better physically," he said, choosing his words carefully, "that you always get a phone call. Is someone monitoring you?"

"I don't think that's any of your business."

"Of course it's my business. It's my lingerie. Tell me how it's working for you."

"Well," she said. "It's kept me from getting too close to you."

"And here I thought it was because you simply didn't like me."

"I like you," she murmured to the door between them. "That's the problem."

Bianca pressed her ear to the door, the champagne glass still balanced in her hand, and listened as he walked away. Blowing out her breath, she set down her glass and quickly finished changing. When she was done, she opened the door and eased out into the main compartment of the airplane. There, she found a lavish picnic lunch—billionaire style—laid out on a buffet. There was caviar and more champagne and puff pastries and small skewers of beef on a stick and fresh fruit and lush salads.

"Please, let's enjoy a nice meal together." Thomaz waved at the spread. Bianca picked up a bone-china plate and loaded up. Thomaz followed behind her, looking refreshed in expensive designer jeans and a crisp, white button-down shirt opened at the collar and rolled up at the sleeves.

They sat near the windows where they could gaze out at the verdant vegetation that was Brazil. As they ate, he told her about his country, its history, traditions, cultures and people.

She listened, absorbing every word. Then he stopped talking and studied her.

"Why are you so afraid to have fun, *bonita?*" he asked.

She shrugged.

"You were hurt." He stared into her as if he could see the depths of her soul.

Oh, God, was she that easy to read?

"Who was he, *bonita?*"

The urge to tell him everything welled up inside her,

but she squashed it. Sharing secrets led to intimacy, and she was having enough trouble fighting her desires. She couldn't look at him any longer and glanced away. "I don't like to talk about it."

Thomaz reached out to cup his fingers under her chin and forced her to look up at him. "Whatever happened, I am not that man."

"I get that, but I've been burned."

"So you wear my underwear to keep me at arm's length."

"I do."

"Who's monitoring you?"

She explained about Izzy and Emma and Madison.

"If I were to give you the five hundred dollars to cover your bet would you stop wearing your so-called chastity belt?" he murmured.

"It's not about the money," she said. "It's about integrity and keeping my head."

"You have to let go of the past, *bonita,* take a chance on the future."

"What are you suggesting, Thomaz? Do you want a long-term relationship with me?" Did she want one with him? The prospect was very scary. She'd been focused on her career for so long, romance had always taken a backseat. Maybe for too long....

He took a deep breath. "I think I do."

That startled her, and Bianca's heart jumped. Could she trust Thomaz? "There are so many obstacles between us. For one thing, I live in America and you live in Brazil."

He nodded. "It is something to consider. I should start looking at real estate in New York."

"No, no. You can't move this quickly. I won't be responsible for a mistake."

"You are not a mistake, Bianca."

"How do you know that?"

"I do not know. I just feel. It's the Brazilian way."

"Well, I'm not Brazilian and this is all moving way too fast for me."

He reached out and splayed a hand over her heart. "You are Brazilian where it counts."

Bianca exhaled sharply.

"But I see I've frightened you. You are accustomed to denying your feelings."

He was right on that score.

"I need time," she whispered.

"We don't have much time."

He was right about that, too.

Thomaz lowered his head.

Bianca knew he was going to kiss her. She didn't resist. Why didn't she resist? This was wrong on so many levels. There was a huge list of reasons she should not allow this to happen.

He dragged her into the kiss, his fervent breath slipping with rousing swiftness into her eager mouth. The fragrance of his hair, musky and dark, stirred her senses. His tongue tasted of cool ocean breezes and the ripe tang of summer. His hands moved with a raw intensity that burned through the skimpy material of her dress, leaving her dizzy. His fingers caressed the underside of her chin. Her temperature soared, flooding her veins with a shivery heat.

Abruptly she turned her back to him and fixated on the view outside.

"Bonita," he murmured, his tongue rimming her earlobe, his hands moving to her waist, driving her mad as he wove them up and down the sides of her body.

His inquisitive index finger explored the groove behind her neck, stroking slowly downward. Immediately, her skin flushed and her heart rate quickened.

Calm down. Take a deep breath. Clear your head.

"Thomaz—" she whispered.

His laugh interrupted her. "Stop thinking. You think too much. Dig down and touch the Brazilian inside you. Feel, *bonita, feel.*"

Firm hands gripped her shoulders, turned her back around, and Bianca stared into his mirthful black eyes.

"Ah, my poor Bianca, therein lies her problem," he said, his fingertips gliding from the curve of her jaw to her throat and on to her cleavage. "You have thought so hard for so long that you have forgotten how to feel. Let me teach you."

His fingers hovered over the top button of her blouse, his palms grazing her breasts. A heated flush of sensual awareness washed over her and her skin ignited. For one heedless moment she had the reckless desire to mold her body against his, grind her hips against his pelvis.

But then her cell phone rang, and she knew without looking at the caller ID that it was one of her friends calling to tell her she was on the verge of losing the bet. She pulled away from him to answer it. She could not lose.

THOMAZ couldn't sleep. Something had come over him at Iguaça Falls when he'd heard Bianca's carefree laughter as their boat had bounced across the choppy water.

He'd known that his desire for her went far deeper than the need for sex. But now he imagined her in his arms, not during sex, but afterward, snuggled up next to him, whispering words of love.

She was the one he'd been waiting for, and he didn't have to wait for Philippe's report to know it. Now that he'd found her, he was alarmed to discover she was not so certain about him. How could he love her if she didn't feel for him the things he felt for her? He'd promised to give her time and space but, honestly, he wasn't sure if he was capable of that.

It delighted and confounded him that she was wearing the sexy underwear he'd invented. She wanted him, but didn't want to want him. How could he break through her defenses? How could he make her see that it was safe to let go of her fears and follow her heart? That she could trust him.

He lay in bed, staring up at the ceiling, imagining Bianca curled in his arms. The sweet, feminine scent of her filling his nostrils. He could feel the soft texture of her hair on his skin, could taste the lips he yearned to kiss.

No matter what he'd told her, he could not stay away from her. If he did, she would only talk herself out of the thing she wanted most, but was too afraid to have.

Determined to make her his, he flung back the covers, got out of bed, dressed quickly, then grabbed the keys to the Ferrari and went to her.

BIANCA lay wide awake staring at the digital clock on the bedside table in her hotel room. All she could think about was Thomaz. She was getting in too deep. She knew it, and yet she couldn't stop herself from falling. She had to get away from him or she was going to succumb to the feelings he stirred in her. First thing in the morning, she was going to call her boss and tell him she'd been unsuccessful. That she needed to come home early. The idea made her cringe. How could she run away when she was so close to the brass ring? She'd worked hard to get where she was and she was just going to walk away from it because she couldn't control a few sexy feelings? That was stupid.

A knock sounded on her door. Concerned, she threw back the covers and padded to the door to peek out the peephole. There stood Thomaz looking extremely agitated.

Her stomach pitched to her feet at the same time her heart soared.

"Bianca," he said. "Please open the door."

She shouldn't. It was dumb. It was as bad as what she'd done with Richard, but Bianca couldn't help herself. She flung open the door.

Thomaz rushed across the threshold and scooped her up into his arms. The next thing she knew, the door was slamming closed behind him and he was kissing her with a ferocity she'd never experienced. It was a kiss that shouted, *you are mine and I am yours, we belong together and everything else be damned.*

And she melted.

So much for her steel will. So much for her career. All she wanted was Thomaz. Helplessly, she linked her arms around his neck and pulled his head down to deepen the kiss. He groaned low in his throat, his hands busily sliding over her body.

His mouth was a branding iron, hot and possessive, claiming her as his own. And how she loved being claimed!

"Thomaz," she murmured. Her heart fluttered. Her stomach felt jittery. Anticipation mingled with anxiety and hope and excitement.

His hands became gentle, sweeping over her body, touching her through her clothes in all the right places. Instantly, she was wet. If someone had told her a week ago that she'd be feeling the kind of things she was feeling, Bianca would have told them they were nuts. Desire, passion, hunger and unstoppable need. She was not the kind of woman who fell easily into love.

Um, you did it with Richard last year.

No, that wasn't true. She hadn't been in love with Richard. She'd felt nothing like the power surging through her now as Thomaz lightly nibbled her earlobe. She and Richard had had a lot in common. She'd been comfortable with him—although that had turned out to be a mistake.

But what if the same thing was happening with Thomaz? A dark voice whispered in the back of her mind, *How do you know you can trust these feelings? How do you know you can trust him?*

She didn't, and therein lay the risk. Bianca wasn't much of a gambler. She led a quiet life, didn't do anything out of the ordinary. The trip on the speedboat underneath the waterfalls had been the most daring—and exhilarating—thing she'd ever done.

Until now.

Until Thomaz.

His lips drank from hers, a bee to a succulent flower. She opened her mouth and let him in, allowed his slow exploration.

There was nothing hurried about the man. Everything he did was purposeful and leisurely. One hand softly stroked her spine, roving up and down the soft material of her lingerie. The other hand held her head still while he kissed her deeper and deeper.

A heated rush of longing pushed through her. She felt her heart skip a beat and her entire body flush. Her breathing came in short, shallow pants. Soon, one of her friends would be calling, probably Emma, to talk her out of this.

"Thomaz," she whispered. "Could you excuse me for a moment?"

"Sure," he said, "but I won't take another breath until you return."

She smiled at him. "I just need to reprogram the access code to my...your..."

"Sex toy." He trailed a hand over the bodice of the chastity belt he'd created.

"Yes."

"You'll lose the bet with your friends."

"I don't care," she said boldly.

His eyes widened and his laugh was hearty, then he lowered his voice and whispered, "Do you want to play a game?"

"What is the game?" she whispered.

"Catch me if you can."

"What are the rules."

"Give me your new access code." He waved in the direction of the GPS device programmed into her underwear. "You leave the hotel and when you're thirty minutes away, turn on the tracking device and I'll come after you," he said in an urgent rush, as if he hadn't even finished thinking the words before saying them aloud.

Goose bumps fled over her body at the thought of his provocative game. "Is this how a woman gets to a one-hour orgasm?"

"It is a step in the right direction, *bonita*." His smiled widened.

Like flotsam being swept over Iguaçu Falls, she was lost in the powerful tidal wave of raw energy she saw in Thomaz's eyes.

"I will find you," he murmured. Gently he kissed her once more, then left her standing alone in the hotel suite.

Now was her chance to reconsider. To put a damper on her errant impulses. She could just lock her door, go to bed and forget all about Thomaz and his wicked little game.

But Bianca didn't want to do that. She wanted to play. For the first time in her life, the studious workaholic wanted to throw it all away for the promise of physical pleasures. Sucking in her breath, she purposely flicked the switch on the little control box nestled in the lining of her underwear and changed the access code. Then she quickly got dressed and hurried out into the street.

There was some kind of festival going on. Loud music, lots of dancing, merriment of all kinds. Couples held hands. Many people were in costume. Some wearing masks. The smell of Brazil was in the air, rich and intoxicating. She imagined her mother growing up on the streets of Rio and she felt a twinge of empathy. Now she understood why her parents had been so protective of her when she was growing up. They'd known of the dangers lurking. They'd wanted to keep their children safe. But that protective bubble had also kept Bianca from fully experiencing the world. She was a grown woman now. Fully capable of making her own decisions and accepting the consequences.

Blood pumping with excitement, she slipped through the crowd. She took her cell phone from her purse and punched in Thomaz's number. The second he answered, she whispered the sequence of her new access code and then said, "Catch me if you can."

She hung up without another word.

5

BELATEDLY, Thomaz realized he'd made a mistake enticing Bianca to play the game. She was unfamiliar with the streets of Rio and while his hometown was glorious in many ways, it did possess a scary underbelly. If you knew what places to stay away from, you would be fine. But an American in certain areas of Rio was a glowing target. Good thing she at least looked Brazilian. Anxiety twisted his throat. He got out his cell and tried to phone her back, to call it off, but the phone went to voice mail. She was playing to the letter of the game. He had to search for her without help.

He hadn't thought about how crowded the streets would be during the festival. How easy it would be to lose her in the throng. How quickly she could get into trouble. All he had was the access code to her GPS tracking. He would find her. He had to find her. He'd been a damned fool to instigate this game. He'd been thinking with his dick and not with his head or his heart. He turned on the tracking device and a green glowing blip appeared on his screen. She'd already made it to Ipanema. On the beach. In the moonlight. All alone. Running from him.

His hunter's instinct kicked in and he was immediately

on the move, getting into his car, navigating the streets as fast as he could in the congestion. He docked the tracking device on the dashboard of his car where he could watch her every move from the corner of his eyes. She was headed west on the beach. He could cut her off if he turned left at the next street. Thomaz's pulse accelerated. His mouth grew dry. His palms were slick on the steering wheel. His eyes constantly darted from the road to the tracking device.

The green blip that was Bianca stopped suddenly. She didn't move for several seconds. A full minute passed. Thomaz was hung up at a red light.

Another minute passed. Her location still didn't change.

Why had she stopped? Had she been accosted on the beach? His mind created a thousand dark scenarios and he viciously cursed himself for his stupidity. Nothing was worth putting her safety at risk.

The light stayed red.

Thomaz didn't care about getting a ticket. All that mattered was getting to Bianca. He zoomed around the car in front of him, ran the red light and almost got side-swiped by a car. The driver saluted him with an obscene gesture. Thomaz didn't even see it.

He bolted toward the beach. His heart a hammer in his chest, his gaze glued to the unmoving blip.

He could see Ipanema. He pulled his sports car haphazardly to a stop on the side of the road, yanked the tracking device from the dashboard and just started running toward the image on the screen.

He found her lying on the beach. Oh, God, he prayed, please let her be okay. "Bianca!" he cried.

She sat up. "I decided I didn't want to run from you. So I lay down here on the beach to look up at the stars. How brilliant they are in the night sky. Do you know how long it's been since I took the time to stargaze?"

Seeing her unharmed, the edgy rush of adrenaline dispersed, leaving his hands shaking, his thoughts scattered, his nerves jittery. "You're okay."

She looked surprised. "Of course I'm okay. Why wouldn't I be?"

He rushed to her, overwhelmed by emotions. He felt relief and gratitude and lust and happiness. So much happiness. "I shouldn't have sent you out alone on your own at night."

"Why not? I'm from New York. I can handle myself."

Yes, yes, she could. He gathered her into his arms, brought her up close against his chest, covering her face in kisses.

"Thomaz? What's wrong?"

"Rio can be a rough place. She is a savage beauty. I imagined awful things happening to you."

"You're trembling."

"I was worried."

"I wasn't," she assured him. "I knew you were watching over me. That you'd come for me."

"You can trust me, *bonita*." He breathed, awed by her trust, especially after she'd admitted she'd been burned badly before. It meant something special, her trust.

"I do," she said as if surprised to realize it herself.

"Did you know your hot little body has been haunting my dreams?" he whispered. "Whenever I close my eyes I can feel your bare skin against mine, taste the sweet nectar of your lips, hear the soft sounds of your pleasure."

His words caused her chin to shoot up and her eyes to narrow. He wasn't surprised by her reaction. She was so easy to ruffle. Thomaz suppressed a smile of amusement. Bianca might think that he was laughing at her, and he was most certainly not. It's just that she made him want to smile. All the time.

"Please," he murmured. "Come to my home with me. Stay the night."

Bianca wrapped her arms around his neck, gave him a soft kiss and whispered, "Why do you think I let you catch me?"

HALF AN HOUR later, they arrived at his palatial home. She probably should have taken the time to notice the modern mansion, but she had eyes only for Thomaz.

He led her by the hand up the spiral staircase to a huge loft bedroom with wide plate-glass windows overlooking the ocean.

Near the window, covered in moonlight streaming silvery-white through the glass, sat a pedestal bed. Thomaz stopped near the bed and pulled her into his embrace.

But she was the one to kiss him, letting Thomaz know they were equal partners in this. Driven by blinding need, she stripped his suit jacket from his broad shoulders and started undoing the buttons of his crisp, white dress shirt.

He took over the kiss, holding her steady with his hands as his tongue explored.

She wriggled against him, absorbing his heat, and ran her palms underneath his shirt, her palms caressing his bare belly.

"Slow down, *bonita,* this is not the way to get a one-hour orgasm."

"I'm beginning to think that's just a myth. You know, like unicorns."

He laughed. "Just you wait and see."

His big hands caressed her body. Butterfly pressure, soft and light. Wherever he touched, she tingled—the hollow spot where her collarbones met, the gully between her breasts, her navel, the apex of her thighs.

Cold, hot, soft, hard, she felt so many contrasting sensations at once.

He kneaded her skin in delicate, rhythmic motions that had her squirming for more. "Tell me what you want, *bonita,* what is your heart's desire?" he murmured.

What *was* her heart's desire? For too long she'd done what was expected of her. She'd poured herself into her work because deep inside she'd believed she was only valued for what she accomplished, not for who she really was. Oddly enough, all that striving and achieving had left her empty inside, so she'd worked even harder to forget that she felt empty.

But things had changed since she'd come to Brazil. *She'd* changed, and Bianca was ready to express her true feelings and ask for what she needed. "I want your mouth on me," she whispered, and touched between her thighs.

"Ah, *bonita,* I am so proud of you," Thomaz said.

And then his mouth was on her in the most disarming way. Hot and wet and glorious.

All thought shut down and she just let herself feel. His palm found her inner thigh, traveled up so his fingers tangled in the springy curls. Her body moved in rhythm with his devastating mouth, his wicked hand. Enchantment stole her brain, as he encouraged her with adoring noises. She drifted in a storm of sensation, her entire body singing his praises.

Time seemed to stretch. He brought her to the edge again and again, but didn't allow her to fall over. He teased her to the point of begging for release, and then he'd back off, slow things down, ease the pressure.

It started in her toes, the beautiful ascent. White-hot wires of sensation thrust into her nerve endings, electrifying her cells, her flesh, her bones. She threaded her hands in his thick, soft dark hair, as the climb escalated, a corkscrew spiral of sheer bliss.

Her release built like a gathering storm, coming in at a slow rumble. Thomaz prolonged her ecstasy with slow kisses, flowering strokes. The storm's wind rushed through her as if she was a hollow tube, pulling her inside out. She vibrated from her toes to her head. On and on and on, caught in a whirlwind of sheer rapture.

Then she hit the eye of the storm—piercingly hot, yet strangely quiet. Sublime paradise. How had he achieved this? Where had he come from, this sex wizard?

She lost control, lost everything, and in the process found herself. It could have lasted an hour or an eternity, because time had ceased to exist. The entire world faded into this complete and utter bliss.

Thomaz roused her after a while, and when she kissed him he tasted creamy and rich and he smelled intoxicating. Her body was covered in a sheen of sweat. His hands skimmed over her body until her need was raw and tumultuous again. His tongue thrust past her teeth, firing her urgency.

"I want…" she gasped. "I want, I want…"

"Yes?"

"To feel you buried inside of me."

She heard the sound of a condom wrapper tearing open, then his hands tenderly brushing her thighs. She dropped her legs wide, giving him full access to her. Nothing hidden. Nothing held back.

He entered her carefully, slowly, and she hissed in a deep breath at his exquisite length pushing against her aching flesh. He stroked her forehead, whispered endearments, kissed her as he slipped in deeper and deeper.

Finally, they were fused. One. Bonded.

Thomaz quickened the pace.

Bianca was gasping and begging for more. She was tumbling, soaring, shuddering.

Who knew, who knew it could feel like this?

Thomaz. That was who.

"Bonita," he cried.

The muscles of her vagina spasmed, squeezing his cock tight. She experienced a release that transcended anything she'd ever had.

In a haze, she heard Thomaz's moans mingling with hers, he shuddered against her, and she saw his face transform into a mask of ecstasy. Inside her he swelled and she felt the hotness of his release as it filled the condom.

His hands went around her waist and he fell to one side of the mattress, rolling her over with him. They lay together panting and spent. Touching, murmuring, kissing softly until they both fell into deep sleep.

BIANCA woke with aches all over her body so sweet she had to smile. What a workout Thomaz had given her. One-hour orgasms indeed. Her grin widened and she sat up. The spot on the mattress next to her was empty and the smell of bacon and eggs wafted into the room.

He was cooking breakfast for her.

Then, she heard the sounds of men's voices, followed by the closing of a door. Did they have visitors?

A white terry-cloth robe had been laid out across a plush leather chair beside the window. She got out of bed, put on the robe and peered out the window just in time to see Philippe climb into his car and motor away. Idly, she wondered what he was doing here so early on a Sunday morning.

The delicious smells got the better of her and she traipsed downstairs, following her nose to the kitchen. It was ultra-modern with gleaming granite counter tops and hardwood floors. But what captured her full attention was the man at the stove, busily flipping pancakes.

"Good morning, *bonita*," he greeted her with a smile.

She started across the room toward him, her heart filled with joy, when she bumped into the countertop and knocked a hand towel to the floor. Something had been underneath the towel and it hit the ground with a flat, weighted sound.

She looked down and saw a black folder with some loose documents that had fallen out. She bent to pick them up, but froze halfway down as she realized what they were.

It was an investigative report including a photograph of her. She was the subject of an investigation? Bianca blinked. What was this?

She reached for the papers, not wanting to believe what she was seeing. Clutching them in her hand, she raised her head to meet Thomaz's gaze. The guilty expression on his face told the entire tale.

"You had me investigated."

He nodded, looking miserable.

"Is that what Philippe was doing here? Did he bring this to you?"

"He is a cop," Thomaz acknowledged, shifting his feet.

The bacon was starting to burn; the acrid smell permeated the room.

"But why?"

He clinched his jaw. "I was falling for you, *bonita*, and I had to be sure you weren't a gold digger. You have to understand my position. I am a wealthy man and—"

She cut him off. "Have you read it?"

He nodded. "It says that you tried to steal an advertising campaign from a rival firm, but they were able to present it before you could. They reported you to your boss and it went on your record."

Bianca froze, chilled to the bone. "It was the other way around," she said. "He stole it from me, but if I'd tried to protest, I would have had to tell them all the embarrassing details. That I met a man and in a very short time he turned my head. I lost my focus. He was very charming. A lot like you. He seduced me with lavish gifts and excellent food."

"You don't need to explain."

"Apparently I do." She tossed the papers on the counter. "He told me I was beautiful, that I was the one he'd been waiting for and I believed him. I fell head over heels. I thought…I thought." How dumb she'd been. Believing in the fantasy. "I trusted him, told him about my work, and he stole my campaign. When we got back to the States I discovered he'd lured away my biggest client and lodged a complaint that I'd tried to steal his idea. I was almost fired over it. You can believe either me or this report. I don't really care which."

"I believe you." He stepped toward her, but she held out a palm to stop him.

"Don't," she said. "Just don't. I was so stupid. I thought last night meant something. I finally let down my guard and I chose to trust you, but for all your big talk about trust, you couldn't trust me, now could you?"

"Bianca, please," he pleaded.

She couldn't believe she'd let herself fall for him. Of course this could never work. The man lived in a mansion. He was so rich he had to have his dates investigated. She had no business with a man like him. Shaken all the way to her soul, Bianca knew she couldn't tell him what she felt for him. If she said she was in love with him, he'd never let her go.

"You don't have to worry, Thomaz. I'm not after your money. For me, this was nothing but a good lay."

Bianca.

No matter how hard he tried, Thomaz could not stop thinking about the woman who'd stolen his heart. He had no idea how it had happened or precisely when she'd sneaked past his defenses, but he was one-hundred-percent in love. And she thought of him as nothing more than a fling.

Thomaz didn't miss the irony. For years he'd avoided commitment, complications, any real responsibility, and now, because of Bianca, he wanted the whole messy, complex thing. Marriage, kids, happily-ever-after. Everything his parents had had, but that Thomaz had shied away from because he feared the pain that came with losing what you prized most.

He'd done everything he could to forget the past and not worry about the future, but now he couldn't keep his mind from the future. With Bianca. His mind was drawn again and again to her. He couldn't eat—he'd lost six pounds since she'd flown home. He couldn't sleep—he'd wake in the middle of the night in his big house and stare at the empty spot in his bed. He no longer took any joy in his hobbies.

He tried everything he knew to break the spell, throwing himself into his favorite activities—dancing the samba until dawn, playing polo, racing his speedboat over the ocean waves, driving his Ferrari way too fast.

But nothing could soothe the loneliness he felt deep inside his soul. All the pursuits he'd once enjoyed seemed so shallow, so purposeless. How had he managed to fall in love with a woman who lived a world away? A woman who'd made it quite clear she was only interested in the temporary physical pleasures they'd shared.

His secretary brought him the sales figures from America and he saw that the lingerie line was racking up impressive sales based on Bianca's strategy to market it as a sex toy for the hip, young, urban professional woman. But all he could think about was how she had made it happen. And that she'd conceded the bet with her friends. For him.

Bianca.

Thomaz looked at her picture that had come in the report Philippe had assembled and took a deep breath. *How in the hell am I ever going to get over you?*

SEVERAL weeks after returning from Brazil, Bianca sat in her boss's office. The sleek Madison Avenue offices of Stillman, Burke and Hollister were commonly abuzz with activity, but today there was added excitement in the air. Four weeks after they'd launched the campaign for Thomaz Santos's Catch Me if You Can lingerie line, they'd gotten the sales figures and the results were toast-worthy. Which was why Bianca's bosses had cracked open a bottle of champagne and invited her into Stillman's hallowed office.

"To a job well done," Roger Burke said and lifted his glass.

"To a job well done," everyone else echoed and clinked the rims of their champagne flutes.

They drank, and then Carl Stillman cleared his throat. "Honestly, Bianca, after what happened last year, we weren't sure you were the right person for the job, but you proved us wrong."

Bianca cringed. If her bosses only knew what had happened in Rio, she'd be getting fired, not accolades.

"Thomaz Santos wrote a glowing letter, singing your praises. You've got quite an admirer in our Brazilian client."

"Thank you, sir." Thomaz had given her a positive review? After the way they'd left things, she was surprised. "It was a delight working for Mr. Santos."

Carl cast a glance at the door to his office, then looked back at Bianca. "After your performance, we were going to offer you a promotion…"

Her heart skipped a beat. "Were?"

"It has come to our attention there's another offer on the table, and you might want to consider them both before making a decision."

Bianca frowned. Another offer? What were they talking about? "Sir, I'm afraid I'm a bit confused—"

She got no further before the conference door opened and Thomaz walked in. His face was expressionless, his wavy hair combed back off his forehead. What was he doing here?

Her heart jumped, suddenly flooded with hope. She was so busy staring at him that she barely registered the fact that everyone else was slipping out the door. The last person pulled it shut behind them, leaving her and Thomaz all alone.

No sooner did the door close than she was seized in his arms and he kissed her with merciless abandon. Hot tingles of sensation rushed to every place in her body that remembered what Thomaz had taught her—how to relax, let go and revel in pleasure. He kissed her for a solid five minutes, holding her tightly as if she was the most precious thing on earth.

Finally, he pulled back so he could look her in the eyes.

She gazed up at him, unable to believe this was really happening. That he was here in New York, his arms wrapped around her, the taste of him sweet on her tongue.

His palms came up to cradle each side of her face and he

stroked her cheeks with his thumbs. His eyes glowed with tender emotions. Could it be, did she dare hope it might be...*love?*

"You're here," she said.

"I'm here," he assured her.

"Why?"

"Do you really have to ask?" he murmured.

"Yes, yes, I do."

"I'm here for you."

"Because of the increased sales figures?"

"No, though I'm glad of that," he said, "and I have no doubt it was all your doing."

Bianca flushed with pride. "I worked hard."

"I know."

"So why did you come to New York?"

He playfully swatted her fanny.

"Hey! What was that for?"

"The 'good lay' thing."

Bianca grinned and wriggled against him. "Well, it was good."

Thomaz growled low in his throat, dipped his head and raked his teeth gently along her throat. His mouth sent shivers of raw desire shuddering throughout her body. "You lied," he said. "I was much more to you than that."

"Look at the ego on you."

"Look at the mouth on you," he said and went in for another kiss.

"Thomaz." She sighed, giving herself over to sensation.

After thoroughly kissing her, Thomaz put his hands on both of her arms and stepped away so he wouldn't be tempted and get carried away again before he could say what he'd come here to say. It wasn't easy. He'd never spoken those words before to anyone other than his parents.

But as he took in Bianca's dear face, he knew she was the one he hadn't even realized he'd been waiting for. So long, playboy lifestyle. Goodbye, doubts and fears. Adieu what used to be. There was a whole new life waiting for him. A life he hadn't even dared to dream of before Bianca.

"Bonita," he whispered. "You are in my blood, in my heart, in my soul." He saw the emotions play across her face, knew she felt them, too.

"Why me? Why now?"

"Other than the fact I'm madly in love with you?"

Bianca inhaled sharply.

"That's right. I love you. I love your dogged intensity and the way you don't let me get away with anything. I love your energy and that you have enough stamina to keep up with me. I love your adventurous nature, how you're willing to try things you've never tried before and you keep an open mind. I love how self-reliant you are, how you're committed to your goals. And I love how you give me the freedom to do my own thing, even when I no longer want that freedom."

"What are you saying, Thomaz?"

"I'm saying I want commitment. I want to settle down. It's time. I'm no longer afraid to take a chance, to grow up, to risk pain in order to get the greatest pleasure of all—love. I love you, Bianca and I'm asking you to give me a chance to prove it. I'll do whatever it takes."

"Oh, Thomaz." Bianca breathed. Then she said what she'd been longing to say for weeks. "I love you, too."

And then there were three....

NEVER ENOUGH

1

*Madison's banking on finding amore, but what about
true love…?*

JAKE STRICKLAND pushed the heavy, black-framed glasses
up on his nose, peering through the nonprescription lenses
at the Power Point presentation projected on the wall of the
main tiki hut. Damn things kept sliding down and it was
all he could do to keep himself from yanking the glasses
off. Playing the role of orchid-loving geek was harder than
it looked.

"You know what they say about the amore orchid?"
whispered Bunk Jones, the seventyish guy sitting next to
him.

Bunk was dressed much like Jake in a Hawaiian-print
shirt, khaki cargo pants and hiking boots. The old dude
had started yapping at him on the long bus ride in from
the San Jose airport and had apparently decided they were
going to become bosom buddies. Jake had done his best to

shake him, but it was a small group and there weren't too
many places to hide in the Costa Rican compound.

Jake didn't ask, but Bunk told him anyway. "Legend
has it that the amore orchid emits such potent pheromones
that whenever you smell it, you have an irresistible urge to
make love."

"What?" Jake jerked his head around to stare at the
wizened fellow.

Bunk nodded solemnly. "Yep, it's true."

"So this orchid is like, what? Floral Viagra?"

He shrugged. "I'm just sayin'…"

"Is that why you're here?" Jake asked. He really didn't
want to think about Bunk being on the prowl, but he supposed old dudes needed love, too. Hey, he wasn't getting
any himself. He'd been going through a dry patch of late,
and this nerdy getup, complete with pocket protector and
unkempt hair wasn't going to help.

"Is that so wrong?" Bunk asked.

"Far be it from me to judge," Jake said. "We've all got
our reasons to be on this trip." *Some of them nobler than
others.*

"I like studious, scientific women, and they tend to
gravitate toward these things." Bunk waved a hand.

He was using an orchid-hunting group as a dating service? Jake scanned the scant pickings and shrugged. To
each his own.

"What about that one over there?" Bunk used his chin
to point at a woman in her mid-twenties sitting on a stool
at the front of the building beside the podium. "She looks
interesting."

The woman was dressed in a style that Jake would only
describe as "mitts-off-the-merchandise-buster." She had
on baggy black jeans, a gray sweatshirt with *Columbia*
printed across the front and a pair of hiking boots. Her

hair was jet-black and fell to her shoulders, Cleopatra-style. She wore skinny, red-framed rectangular glasses and no jewelry whatsoever. Her skin was notebook-paper pale. A sheen of pink lip gloss rode her lips and her mascara was the same color as her hair. Her eyes, from what he could see of them behind those glasses, were chocolate-brown.

Weirdly, his pulse skittered. Why on earth would he feel a sudden attraction? She was certainly not his type. "She's too young for you," he told Bunk.

"Not for me. I got my eyes on Lucinda." Bunk indicated a silver-haired woman in the first row. "I meant for you."

"Nah, she's not for me."

"Why not? You in a relationship?"

"No way," Jake said. "I'm footloose and fancy free."

"Ah." Bunk smiled. "You're one of those."

It seemed like an indictment, and this from a coot old enough to be Jake's grandfather. "I'm one of those what?"

"The love 'em and leave 'em kind."

Jake was about to argue, then he shut his mouth. He didn't intentionally set out to love 'em and leave 'em, but whenever a woman started talking about taking their relationship to the next level—i.e., commitment—Jake's feet got twitchy.

"You're right," Bunk agreed. "She's too much woman for you."

"Who? Emo girl?"

"Emo?" Bunk looked confused.

"Never mind." Jake waved a hand. "What makes you think she's too much woman for me?"

"That woman…" Bunk nodded as if he knew everything. "She needs a man who'll stick around and find out exactly what's going on in that brain of hers. She's sharp as a tack. You can see that right off the bat."

Huh? Jake stared at Emo girl. In that moment, she raised her head.

Their eyes met, and for one second he could have sworn he saw surprise in her eyes, as if she knew him. But in an instant the look was gone and she simply glared at him like he was getting on her last nerve. Jake was the first one to break eye contact—not his usual MO.

"Yep." Bunk chuckled. "She's too much woman for the likes of Mr. Love 'em and Leave 'em."

"Stop calling me that," Jake snapped, irritated.

"Hey, if the shoe fits…" Bunk shrugged. "Me, I'm going up there to talk to Lucinda."

And then the old man was gone, ambling down the grass aisle to the front row. He leaned in to say something to Lucinda who smiled up at him and scooted over so Bunk could take the seat next to her. Jake had to give the old man props for moving fast.

Just then, a man stalked through the back door of the tiki hut and up to the podium. He introduced himself as Professor Hampton from Columbia University and turned to Emo girl perched on the stool. "And this is my number-one research assistant, Madison Garrett. She's doing her doctoral dissertation on the amore orchid."

Madison raised a hand and smiled at the group, but when her eyes met his again, the welcoming smile disappeared. What? She didn't like him? That was unusual. Women almost always liked him. At least until they figured out he wasn't the kind to stick around.

Professor Hampton went into detail about the research project he and his team were engaged in. They wanted to find the amore orchid—which was rumored to exist only in Costa Rica—and get it listed on the endangered species list.

If the group only knew he was working for an orchid

collector in Taiwan, his goose was cooked and he'd end up
on the wrong side of a lynch mob. Clearly these people took
their orchids seriously. He didn't get what the big deal was.
It was just a flower. Jake had no real vested interest in the
orchid itself. All he cared about was the sweet paycheck
Tao Liu offered.

Two weeks ago, Tao Liu had approached Jake at Joe's
Bar and Grill, his favorite hangout in L.A., and told him
about Professor Hampton's Costa Rican expedition. Jake
had never smuggled orchids before. For the most part, his
enterprises were legal, if perhaps sometimes a tad unethi-
cal, but his job gave him flexibility and the ability to see
the world on someone else's dime.

Obtaining the orchids for Liu just seemed like a quick
way to make a buck and right now he was really hard-up
for cash. Not for himself, but for Joe, the man who'd taken
him off the streets and given him a home when he was a
twelve-year-old runaway. Tough economic times had put
Joe behind the eight ball and he was about to lose the
bar and grill. The place was all Joe had. Without it, Jake
didn't think his surrogate father would survive. It was time
for him to give back to the only person who'd ever really
believed in him.

Of course, it was going to require a bit of subterfuge.
Like maybe cozying up with Miss Madison Garrett. The
idea wasn't repulsive. Beneath the glasses and the frumpy
clothes, she was actually not bad-looking. Why did she
hide herself behind those glasses and that dark sheaf of
thick hair?

"The amore orchid is very rare and there are collectors
who will stop at nothing to have one—and that includes
hiring soldiers of fortune to beat us to the punch and steal
them."

Jake forced himself not to slink down in his seat. Hey,

he didn't consider himself a soldier of fortune. The term
had such pejorative connotations. He was more daring
adventurer—searching for buried treasure, acting as a
guide in countries with iffy political situations, obtaining useful information for various groups and individuals.
That's how he saw himself. A man who dared go where
others feared to tread.

THE LECTURE ended and the group immediately gravitated
to the wine and cheese buffet set up on one side of the hut.
Madison stood awkwardly in the corner, making her obliga-
tory appearance and waiting for the chance to escape to the
quiet of her hut. She hated these meet-and-greets. Luckily,
the majority of the volunteers were over fifty; she often felt
more comfortable in the company of older people.

Although…there was one guy near her own age. He
wore rectangular framed glasses that were almost identi-
cal to the ones she had on, except where hers were red, his
were black. His hair was shaggy, unkempt, and a pocket
protector filled with pens peeked from his shirt pocket.
Nothing suspicious about any of that. Almost every male
in the place—including her professor—looked similar.

No, what stuck out about this guy was the way he carried
himself. Not slump-shouldered and shy like most introverts,
but rather with razor-straight shoulders, almost military in
stance. He also possessed a smug grin and a way of moving
that shouted, "I'm the cock of the walk."

He was more than he appeared. A guy playing at being
a nerdy geek? Instantly a red flag went up in her mind.

Blowing out her breath to bolster her courage, Madison
strolled over and put a smile on her face. Should she treat
him like the introvert he seemed to be or just go ahead and
shoot for the ego he couldn't cover up?

In the end, her own timidity won out. "Hi," she said simply.

A slow, easy grin started at one side of his mouth and slipped to the other, and his eyes held onto hers. Oh, yeah, there was something definitely off about this guy.

But then he quickly dropped his gaze, ducked his head, toed the ground and mumbled, "Hello."

"I'm Madison," she said and boldly thrust out her hand.

"Um…so I heard…" he replied, still keeping his gaze averted, but reaching up at last to take her hand.

The second their palms touched a shot of pure sexual awareness spread down his arms and traveled up hers. The sensation was electric. She'd never felt anything like it.

His eyes widened and he looked as thrown as she was. Quickly, they both dropped their hands.

They stood there, focusing on anything but each other. Madison hooked one arm around the other. "What's your name?"

"Jake. Jake Strickland." He pushed his glasses up.

This time she noticed his thick, work-roughened hands. From gardening? She felt her attraction to him grow. This wasn't normal for her. She wasn't the kind of woman who did anything spontaneously, much less fall in lust, but she couldn't help letting her eyes track from his muscular shoulders—so non-geekish—to his broad chest, waist, narrow hips and… She jerked her gaze away. *For heaven's sake, Madison, don't stare at the man's crotch.*

"Well, Jake Strickland, it's nice to meet you."

"Nice to meet you as well, Maddie Garrett." His shy grin had turned bold again.

"It's not Maddie. It's Madison. No one calls me Maddie."

"Why not?"

"I don't like it."

"Why not?"

"What are you? Three years old?"

"I'm just inquisitive." His smile softened.

Madison's belly churned. She couldn't decide whether to be attracted to him or to be suspicious of him for his conflicting behavior.

"Are you ready for tomorrow?" she asked.

"I am."

"We leave at dawn." She didn't know why she was hanging around, baiting him.

"I'll be ready."

"Be sure to bring the supplies listed on the hiking guide in your welcome kit. It can get pretty hairy out there."

"I've been in a few jungles," he said. "I know what to bring."

Now *that* sounded one-hundred-percent cocky. Not at all like something a nerd would say. She narrowed her eyes and was about to start interrogating him about his jungle experience but he preempted her.

"See you in the morning, Maddie." He turned and walked away, leaving Madison more irritated, confused and attracted than she'd ever been in her life.

JAKE let out a deep breath as soon as he ducked around the corner of the hut. He had to be really careful with Madison Garrett. She was as sharp as a shark's tooth, and playing at being a nerd wasn't second nature to him. He was a self-confident guy who normally took the lead with a woman when he was interested, and it had required every bit of willpower he possessed to pretend to be shy and retiring. He didn't think he'd been all that successful. Especially there at the end when she'd been shooting him dirty looks.

Bunk was right about one thing. Pulling the wool over her eyes was not going to be easy.

He was lurking outside the main tiki hut where almost everyone still lingered over drinks and nibbles, trying to plan his course of action, when he saw Professor Hampton and Madison emerge from the back entrance. They stood in the glow from the flickering tiki torches and it seemed as if they were arguing. Keeping to the shadows, Jake crept closer.

"Based on my calculations—" Madison said and then spouted intricate scientific mumbo jumbo about ph balance and soil conditions, optimum temperature range and daylight "—the amore orchid is most likely to be growing on the northern slopes above the San Pablo waterfalls."

"Your calculations are inexact at best since every species of orchid has its own specific conditions for optimal germination. Plus native folklore has the amore orchid growing far south of the San Pablo," Professor Hampton argued.

Hmm, apparently there was tension between the teacher and his student. Jake rubbed his chin pensively and eased closer.

Madison sank her hands on her hips. "You said you'd give my input serious consideration."

"I did, and I decided you're wrong."

Anger crept into her voice. "I don't understand how you can dismiss my work so cavalierly. I have spent three years of my life on this research and—"

"We don't have the time or manpower to go gallivanting off on your wild-goose chase, Madison," he said curtly.

"Wait a minute." She glowered. "Is this about last summer?"

"Of course not," Professor Hampton retorted, but his voice went up an octave.

"It is! You're mad because I broke things off with you and you're punishing me."

"Don't be ridiculous." He snorted.

"You said we were both adults, that you could still work with me. I took you at your word."

"Our little fling meant nothing," Hampton denied.

Ouch. So Hampton and his research assistant had gotten it on last summer and now this horse's ass was taking it out on her when it had gone south. Jake felt a twinge of sympathy. In the light from the full moon Madison looked mad enough to rip open a coconut with her bare hands.

Man, but she was fierce. Jake felt a curious stirring inside him. A sizzle that started in his stomach and sped downward.

"If you take your group south you're not going to find a damn thing," she said.

"What do you mean *your* group?" Hampton scowled. "It's *our* group."

"Not any more it's not. I've spent my entire adult life looking for the amore orchid and I'm not going to be disappointed again. Not when I'm so close. I'm going north to San Pablo. You're free to follow me if you want, otherwise, I'll see you in a week." With that parting shot, Madison turned on her heels, ducked her head and started stalking toward Jake so quickly that he didn't have time to get out of her way, and she ran smack dab into him.

The collision forced all the air from Jake's lungs. "Ooph."

She'd bowled him over. Literally. He was lying on the ground and she was straddling his torso.

He blinked up at her. She stared down at him. He saw in her eyes the same baffled attraction he felt.

Madison uttered an unladylike curse word and sprang to her feet. "What were you doing prowling in the dark?"

"I wasn't prowling," he lied and levered himself to his feet. He splayed a palm to his stomach. Was it pitching because of the impact or because of the full-body contact with Madison?

They stood glaring at each other, neither one of them moving.

"Madison," Professor Hampton's voice was sharp in the darkness. "We have to discuss the logistics of separate expeditions."

"You're being summoned," Jake said.

She swallowed, but didn't look away. "Coming."

Rattled by the chemistry surging between them, Jake said, "You gotta come, I gotta go." He heard how that sounded, winced, tried to backtrack. "You gotta go, I've gotta come." Hell, he'd just made things worse. "I mean—"

"Get to your tent," Madison commanded and pointed in the direction of the volunteers' accommodations.

Bossy. He kind of liked that.

"I want to come with you," he said, meaning he wanted to be part of her expedition, but under the circumstances it had a completely different meaning.

She gave him a "go-straight-to-hell" look.

"What I meant to say—"

"I know what you meant to say."

"So can I? Come?"

"Stop saying that word."

He pantomimed zipping his lip.

"Madison?" Hampton called again.

She sent an assessing glance over Jake. "Be packed and ready to go. I'll meet you in the cantina hut at 6:00 a.m.," she hissed, "If you're not there, I leave without you." Then she spun on her heels and stalked away in the darkness.

That's when he knew she liked him, too.

WHY HAD SHE agreed to take that weird Jake Strickland into the jungle with her? Madison wondered as she brushed her teeth and got ready for bed. Especially after she'd caught him eavesdropping on the fight she'd had with Hampton.

But the truth was, even though she was sure her calculations on where to find the orchid were correct, the idea of venturing into the ruggedly beautiful tropical terrain on her own scared the pants off her. She was a scholar, not an adventurer. There might be something off about Strickland, but he looked to be as adventurous as they came and in excellent physical condition.

Unfortunately, she felt a bizarre attraction toward him.

Okay, maybe the attraction wasn't so inexplicable. He had a million muscles, all firm and honed. A strong jaw just begging to be stroked. Eyes the color of cymbidium orchids. A roguish, broken nose that added to rather than detracted from his sex appeal. And besides all that, he smelled good.

Thank heavens she'd worn the chastity belt and taken Izzy's bet. The last thing she needed was a sexual distraction.

Because Strickland was surely that.

Madison crawled into her sleeping bag wearing the silky lingerie designed by Thomaz Santos and tried not to notice how it caressed her skin. She also tried not to think about Jake and his hands slipping beneath the waistband of the panties.

Stop it!

Right. Head in the game. She was in the middle of a turf war with her professor. If she was going to fret about something, that's what she should be fretting about.

She'd known that impossible fling they'd had last

summer had been a big mistake. They'd been in Belize, hunting down a lead on an amore sighting. It had turned out to be just *Dichaea muricaroides*.

Their disappointment had been so great that they consoled themselves in each other's arms. It was stupid. They'd had too much to drink and afterward they'd sworn never to speak of their short-lived affair again, and on the surface it seemed their teacher/student relationship had gone back to normal. But now, Hampton's stubbornness to acknowledge that her theory had merit told her she'd been deceiving herself. He wasn't about to admit she was on to something, even to the point of letting his ego get in the way of the chance to fulfill his quest.

Well, fine. If Hampton was with her when she found the amore, he'd take the credit. This way, *she'd* get it.

Whichever, she had to stop ruminating and get some sleep. She had a big day ahead of her. Who knew? Maybe tomorrow her most cherished dream would come true.

2

MADISON had told Jake to meet her at six because she wanted to leave camp before Hampton and his entourage. When she got to the cantina, Jake was already there, stuffing muffins in his backpack and swilling a cup of coffee. When he saw her, he paused to push his glasses up on his nose and then grinned as if he was truly, madly glad to see her. Suddenly, her pulse accelerated.

"Mornin'," he said in a lazy drawl.

Heightened awareness shot through her and she curled her hands into fists. She moved ahead of him, feeling the silky lingerie she had on shift sexily. She shouldn't have worn the damned thing. It was certainly not wilderness attire, but she'd made that silly bet with her friends, so she'd worn it and turned it on.

She filled her own backpack, shouldered it and headed out of camp. She sensed Jake fall in behind her, but she did not turn her head when she said, "Let's go."

The eastern sky was tinged purple as they trudged into the darkened jungle. Jake came up beside her, walking abreast, even though the narrow path they were on required walking in single file. Palm fronds brushed against their legs and their shoulders made contact.

Madison veered away from him, stumbling over a tree root but she quickly regained her balance. "Why don't you stay behind me?"

"It's more fun being beside you. And it's easier to talk when we're side-by-side."

"But not easier to walk."

"You—" he started, but bit the words off.

She glared at him. "What?"

"Nothing."

"Look, I'm really not much of a talker. I enjoy peace and quiet. So how about we just not have a peppy early-morning conversation."

"You giving me the brush-off?"

"I just want to pay attention to the task at hand," she said. "We're entering a tropical rain forest and the sun isn't even up yet. There's all kinds of wildlife in here, much of it unfriendly to humans."

"You know a lot about Costa Rican wildlife?"

Honestly, nothing more than what she'd read about in guidebooks. Her entire focus had been on finding the amore orchid.

"Why are you here?" she asked.

"I thought you didn't want to talk."

"You don't seem like an orchid enthusiast."

"What makes you say that?"

"For one thing, you're under thirty."

"So?"

"There are very few heterosexual men under the age of thirty who are interested in orchids."

"Well." He cracked a smile. "I'm not your ordinary guy."

She let it go for the moment and eventually, he fell back as they traveled deeper into the jungle, letting her lead. Sunlight slowly began filtering in through the lush vegetation and the sounds of the rain forest were all around them. Exotic birds, the scurrying of small animals, the clicking of insects. It was a vivid green world. Madison took a deep breath of the humid air, sweet with the smell of tropical flowers. She wondered what the amore orchid smelled like. Whether it was as a sensual as everyone claimed.

As if reading her mind Jake asked, "Do you think the rumors about the amore are true?"

"What rumors?" She feigned ignorance, then immediately wondered why she'd done that. If she pretended to be clueless about that legend, that meant he'd have to fill her in, and the last thing she wanted was to talk about sex with Jake. To reverse the challenge she'd inadvertently instigated, she stopped short and he almost plowed into her. She remembered last night, when she'd plowed into *him*. "What was that noise?"

Jake paused, cocked his head. "What noise?"

"Um…I don't hear it now." She started walking again.

"So," he said, "when we find this field of amore orchids are you prepared for the consequences?"

Madison thought of the chastity belt she wore. *You have no idea.* "What? You think one sniff of the orchid will drive me wild and I'll rip your clothes off?"

"A guy can hope." He laughed.

That should have ticked her off, instead she felt flattered. It had been a long time since a guy had flirted this outrageously with her. "Don't be ridiculous. No plant can make a person act out of character."

"Meaning you're not the type of woman who would rip off a stranger's clothes and make love to him in a field of orchids even if you were madly attracted to him."

Honestly, she'd love to make love surrounded by orchids. It was one of her biggest sexual fantasies, but no way was she going to tell this guy that. "I'm not the least bit attracted to you."

"Ha!"

"Ha? What the hell does that mean?"

"You're attracted to me."

"You're full of yourself."

"That doesn't change the fact that you're interested."

"Jeez, the ego. Where'd you get it? Egos Are Us?"

"Witty."

"Thank you. Now could you please stay behind me? You're getting on my nerves."

"Maybe you should be behind me," he said.

"Why on earth would I do that?'

"Because you're about to walk right off the edge of a cliff."

"I am n—"

But she didn't even get the words out of her mouth. One minute she was standing on firm ground, the next second she'd taken a step forward into a thicket of vegetation and the ground just disappeared from underneath her.

MADISON's screams echoed through the forest.

"Holy shit," Jake exclaimed, the hairs standing up on the back of his neck.

One second she'd been arguing with him like she knew what she was talking about, and the next she was sliding headlong down a cliff of tropical vegetation, barreling straight toward a rushing stream several hundred yards below them.

"Hang on, Maddie, I'm coming for you!"

Feeling as though he'd just stepped into the movie *Romancing the Stone,* Jake peered down the incline only to have the ground crumble beneath him. Then he was sluicing down the slick, green plant-chute after her at breakneck speed. Okay, now he knew why she was screaming. It was a damned scary sensation, even for a daring adventurer.

Seconds later, he shot from the muddy flume and landed in the water. Instantly, he was caught up into a powerful eddy that sent him barreling downstream. He sputtered, kicked, tried to shove the wet hair from his eyes to see if he could locate Maddie.

He tried to call out to her, but water filled his mouth. She was bound to be terrified, poor kid. He fought to swim, but his backpack weighed him down. He gulped in a lungful of nasty jungle water and started coughing.

Get yourself together. Shake it off.

Jake blinked, struggled to get his footing. Then— *ouch!*

Something snatched at his hair. He muttered a colorful curse word as he felt himself being dragged.

Then he was lying spread-eagled on the ground underneath a guanacaste tree and Maddie was standing over him looking very pissed off. Her midnight-black hair was plastered to her face and her clothes clung wetly to her body. From his position on the ground, the view wasn't half bad. He liked the way her shirt molded to her breasts, revealing that Maddie was hiding some very nice assets underneath her baggy attire. How had she managed to get out of the water on her own and then turn right around and save his ass? He was at once admiring and puzzled. There was more to this woman than met the eye.

He rolled over onto his side and stayed there, noticing the way her cargo shorts wrapped around her pale thighs. He'd never thought pale was a good color until he saw it on Maddie.

"Get up," she said.

"What are you? A drill sergeant?"

"You're lying in leeches."

"Leeches!" He yelped and got to his feet, slapping himself. "I hate leeches. Get 'em off, get 'em off."

Maddie burst out laughing.

He glared at her. "Leeches are not a laughing matter."

"I lied. It's not leeches, just leaves."

He was so relieved that he wasn't mad. "Why'd you do that?"

"So you'd stop lying there staring up at me with that goofy expression on your face."

"You know how to control a man."

"Thanks for the compliment."

"It was a complaint." He put his palms to his back and stretched.

"You lost your glasses," she said.

"Oh, yeah." He squinted intentionally.

She gave him an odd look.

"How did you manage to hang onto yours?" he asked.

"I grabbed hold of them as soon as I fell. I can't see a thing without them."

He didn't want her to ask him any more glasses-related questions, so he stared up at the cliff that had completely dissolved underneath them. It was a least the length of two football fields away and there was no climbing up it. "Now we have to figure out how the hell to get back on the main trail."

"That does seem to pose a problem," she agreed, following his gaze.

He turned his head to study her. "You're not freaking out."

"Why would I freak out?"

"Most women I've known would."

"You've never known me."

"I'm beginning to see that. But you don't really look like an outdoors girl, either. All the pale skin."

"I can't help it that I'm pale."

"You don't tan?"

"Nope."

"Got vampire lineage?"

She laughed. "I have to wear lots of sunscreen or I burn to a crisp."

"Well, whatever it is, it's working for you."

"Why don't we just take that path?" she asked, ignoring his compliment.

"What path?"

Madison pointed to a faint trail that disappeared into the woods. "I'm just praying it doesn't lead to a jaguar's den or something equally terrifying."

"Well." Jake grinned. "What are we waiting for? Let's get a move on."

THEY'D BEEN hiking for well over two hours when the rain started. Not just a little spattering, either. Not sprinkles or raindrops or summer showers. This was an honest-to-God deluge.

Huge sheets of water poured from a dark sky, drenching them to the skin. At least it washed the mud away. Madison tried to console herself with the logic, but she wasn't up to the challenge. Even though the temperature was warm, the abundant, constant rain made her shiver.

Jake looked as miserable as she felt. They could barely walk against the onslaught. The ground churned to mud beneath their feet. To make their way they had to cling to trees and fronds, anything they could grab onto. It was in the midst of this hell that Jake let out a hoot of delight.

For a moment, Madison thought he might have lost his mind. Especially when he started running. Or rather running, slipping, falling, getting back up and running again.

She searched the jungle trying to see where he was going. And then, through the mass of water and the thicket of greenery, she saw it. A little wooden hut balanced on the top of a rise, almost completely hidden by the trees. The introvert in her worried that someone lived there and they'd be intruding, but her practical side told her to get over her shyness and follow Jake.

He stopped and turned back to her. "Stay here and let me check this out. It might not be safe."

Madison paused. Costa Rica wasn't in political turmoil but some of the neighboring countries were. What if guerillas lived in the hut? Clearly, he'd considered it.

She halted in midstride, rain rolling down her face, and she waited while Jake scaled the slippery hill to the hut. It was a short distance but the trip took him a long time in the muck and the mire. He cut a dashing figure—agile and quick—and her breath caught in her lungs. Oh, yes, he was much more than he seemed.

From the time she was a small kid, she'd been enchanted by stories of swashbucklers and rollicking adventures. She'd cut her teeth on Jules Verne and Edgar Rice Burroughs. She loved Indiana Jones and *Romancing the Stone* and any movie or book fraught with danger and the thrill of the chase. Mainly because she had so little of those elements in her own quiet, bookish life. There might be something not quite right about Jake, but right now she was just going to try and enjoy being part of the adventure.

Several minutes after he entered the hut, Jake appeared on the small ledge that barely qualified as a front porch and waved her up. "C'mon, it's dry in here."

She started up the rise, but couldn't find a decent foothold. How in the world had he managed to climb this? After several minutes of struggling, a rope suddenly appeared in front of her face. She glanced up to see Jake standing above her holding the other end of the rope.

"Grab on and I'll pull you up."

After several minutes of grunting and tugging, Madison hauled herself up over the side of the hill and collapsed on the ground at his feet, breathing like a landed guppy. She was covered in mud and drenched to her soul, but she'd made it.

"Well done," Jake said, and put down a hand to help her rise.

She touched his hand and there it was again, that same spark, that same strike of electricity. It was so powerful she almost lost her balance and tumbled back down over the ledge. But Jake held on to her, drawing her closer.

"Whoa there, Maddie."

She'd always disliked the nickname Maddie. The moniker belonged to a lighthearted person, not a serious scientist. Even when she was quite small she'd insisted everyone call her Madison and she got huffy when any of her friends—usually Izzy—dared call her Maddie.

But when Jake said it, the name sounded like cool water trickling over hot rocks. What was it about the guy that so appealed to her? She didn't believe in love at first sight. Heck, she'd been suspicious of him from the minute she'd laid eyes on him, but there was something about the guy that just pushed all the right sexual buttons inside her and to hell with everything else.

Why?

Don't forget what happened last year when you threw caution to the wind with Hampton. You ended up with regrets. Don't make that same mistake twice.

She wouldn't.

"Let's get inside," Jake said, pulling her even closer. His

breath was warm against her ear and she allowed him to lead her gently inside the hut.

As domiciles went, it was pretty basic. One room. Roof made of palm fronds. A camp stove in one corner. And that was it. Shelter from the weather and really nothing more. But it was dry and relatively free of creatures, although she did spy a couple of click beetles scuttling across the floor. Not exactly the Plaza, but it would do in a pinch.

"Do you have a change of clothes in that backpack?" he asked.

"Yeah."

"There's an outdoor shower on the back porch," he said. "If you want to rinse the mud off."

She did. "Convenient."

"You go first," he offered and waved his hand in a magnanimous gesture.

Madison went to the porch and saw that the "shower" was little better than standing under the spout of an open water tower. Still, it was something. Of course she wasn't going to get naked. Not with Jake inside the hut. She didn't trust him not to peek out at her. And then there was the matter of the lingerie. She couldn't take the damned thing off without notifying her friends first, and she didn't feel inclined to dig out her cell phone and explain her predicament. She'd just have a quick rinse with the lingerie on. Good thing the sensor was encased in a waterproof cover.

"Got a towel?" he asked.

She shook her head. "I didn't think to bring one."

"Don't worry. I've got you covered." He plucked a towel from his own backpack.

The towel smelled of sandalwood soap. She pressed it to her face, then looked over and saw he was holding out a bar of soap. "Were you ever a Boy Scout?"

"Why do you ask?"

"You seem prepared for anything."

His grin widened. "Nope, no Boy Scout here. I told you, I know my way around the jungle."

"A regular Tarzan, huh?"

He pounded on his chest with his fists and made Tarzan noises.

"Okay, that was dorky," Madison said.

"Didn't do a lot for my sex appeal?" He wriggled his eyebrows.

"Zero on a scale of one to ten."

"No more chest pounding. Got it." He grinned.

She was struck again by the paradox of this man. Who was he really? Orchid nerd, or something else entirely?

She couldn't help smiling back, though, as she headed for the porch, soap in hand. She left the towel inside on a hook beside the door and stepped out into the rain. It seemed a bit dumb to shower in a deluge, but she felt grimy. She stripped out of her clothes—save for the underwear— and cast a glance over her shoulder to see if Jake was peering out the door at her. To her disappointment, he was not.

Why are you disappointed? Thank heavens he's not a voyeur.

She turned and busied herself with cleaning up, reminding herself that despite the sparks between them, she didn't know anything about him.

Jake sauntered over to the part of the hut that gave him an eyeful of the shower area. From this vantage point, he could see her, but Maddie wouldn't be able to see him. He watched her shimmy out of her clothes and his heart jackhammered.

Okay, not cool, Strickland. No staring.

But he couldn't seem to help himself. Maddie had a body worth ogling. She didn't get all the way naked and somehow that was even sexier than total nudity. She wore a skimpy little pink-and-white matching bra and panties with some little belt thing that connected the two at the waist.

And what a body! It was even better than he'd suspected. Why did she hide it beneath those baggy clothes?

Jake felt himself harden. *Hold up, fella. She's certainly not on the menu. Especially when you're planning on stealing those orchids out from under her.*

Still he allowed his gaze to rove over Madison, and he realized he was feeling more than simple lust—extreme interest combined with intense curiosity and a strange, bone-deep yearning. Whenever he looked at her he experienced a strange tingling in the area of his heart. What was it about her that so intrigued him? Was it her intelligence? Her sharp wit? The way she didn't put up with his shit?

There might be something to that last part. He was used to women draping themselves all over him. Madison acted as though he wasn't worth her time.

Oh, this is so messed up. You wanting a woman who is just not that into you.

He couldn't remember ever being interested in a woman who had no interest in him. Women were *always* interested in him. That was the problem. He'd been accused of sending out mixed signals. Acting as though he wanted to be close, but then when the relationship started getting serious swinging off to one foreign country or the other, gone for weeks.

If he ever did get serious about a woman, he made sure she understood that he possessed a bad case of wanderlust and there was no cure. Not that he wanted to cure himself of it. Jake loved his life. He was free to come and go as he pleased. Yes, okay, sometimes he did make his money in shady ways. Making off with rare wild orchids for a less-than-scrupulous collector, for instance. But he wasn't doing that for himself. It was to help Joe keep his bar.

He stepped away from the window, not wanting Maddie to catch him ogling her.

The truth was that she was getting to him in a way no other woman had. And it was taking every ounce of self-control—which admittedly wasn't a lot—he possessed not to stalk out on that back porch, yank her into his arms and kiss her until neither one of them could breathe.

Jake wasn't about to do anything that stupid, but his cock was so hard it hurt. She made him crazy.

His feelings were bizarre, surreal. It was like…fate.

Don't be a putz. You don't even know her and she doesn't know you. She'd hate you if she did.

And yet, he couldn't stop wanting her. He imagined her touching him. A phantom caress that electrified every nerve ending in his body. He visualized her long dark hair lightly tickling his bare skin. He could taste her on his tongue—warm, feminine, alive.

Jake shoved a hand through his hair, hauled in a deep breath. A strange panic settled all the way into his bones.

What in the hell was this feeling?

Better question, how could he make it go away?

3

MADISON poked her head through the door and grabbed the towel off the hook. "Turn around."

"Huh?"

"Turn your back, I don't want you to see me."

"Fine." Jake sighed and spun around.

Madison slipped inside and wrapped the towel around herself. The chastity belt was plastered to her skin. She whisked the towel over her body, getting as dry as she could, then tied the towel around her wet hair, tucking it into a turban. Next, she tiptoed across the floor to her backpack. "Keep looking at the wall."

"What are you so afraid of, Maddie? That I'll rip that skimpy little lingerie off and have my way with you?"

"You looked!"

"No, I didn't. I've been dutifully staring at the wall."

"You looked when I was outside."

"Hey, you never said I couldn't look while you were outside."

"Pervert."

"Prude."

Madison gasped. The audacity of the man.

"Will you tell me just one thing?" he asked.

"No."

"Is that thing you're wearing what I think it is?"

"What do you think it is?"

"Some kind of chastity belt?"

"How do you know that?"

"I once had this girlfriend who liked to play hard to get—"

"I don't really need the blow-by-blow details of your love life, thank you very much."

"You asked."

"Sorry, my mistake." Madison yanked her spare pair of jeans from her backpack and wriggled into them. Then she fished out a plain white oversize T-shirt and pulled that on as well, being careful not to knock the towel off her head in the process. "Okay, you can turn around."

Jake pivoted to face her, that ubiquitous grin on his face. Did the man ever stop smiling? "Why do you wear clothes that are too big for you when you have such a smokin'-hot body?"

"Maybe so assholes such as you don't leer at me."

"Hey, I'm not an asshole."

"No? Could have fooled me."

"Why don't you like me?"

She shrugged. "I know your type. You breeze through life on your own terms, not caring who you hurt."

"You talking about Professor Hampton?" Jake asked. "Did you two have a fling that went bad?"

Madison wrinkled her nose. "No. Yes. Maybe. Sort of."

"Which is it?"

"It's not just Hampton."

"No?"

"I have a tendency to be attracted to ne'er-do-wells."

"Ne'er-do-wells?" Jake laughed. "Who are you? Jane Austen?"

Madison went on the defensive. "What's wrong with Jane Austen? She's my favorite writer."

"There's nothing wrong with Jane Austen if you're Jane Austen. You however, are Maddie Garrett."

"Madison," she corrected.

"So tell me about the ne'er-do-wells."

"Why?"

He waved a hand at the rain slanting hard in front of the hut. "Not much else to do."

"Besides Hampton?"

"Besides him. How many were there?"

"That's a personal question."

He shrugged.

"Four actually," she admitted, not knowing why she was doing so. "If you count my father. He was the kind of guy who promised you the sky, then disappeared on your sixth birthday and would only show up every couple of years or so to take you to Coney Island, assuming that would make up for everything."

"Ouch. I'm sorry."

She shrugged. "I'm over it."

"Are you really?"

"Yes," she said firmly. She had gotten over her anger at her father. In fact, she'd forgiven him, and she saw him more often now than she had when she was a kid. But she still feared she was susceptible to good-looking, dark-haired men with winsome smiles.

"And the second one?"

"High-school sweetheart. The usual story. Captain of the football team. Couldn't believe he was interested in me. Caught him with the head cheerleader. Learned he was dating me to get me to do his homework."

"And the third?"

"Fiancé."

"Left you at the altar?"

"No, I left *him* after I realized I was trying to tame a man who couldn't be tamed."

"A twist. I like it."

"I'm not looking for your approval."

"No?"

"Not in the least."

"The fourth?" he prodded.

"Short-term fling. Rebound from the fiancé."

Jake shrugged. "Good enough for me. I guess it's my turn at the shower." He held out his hand.

"What?"

"My soap and towel. Could I have them back?"

"Oh. Yeah." She found the soap she'd left sitting on her bag, unwound his towel from around her hair and gave both items to him. "I'm afraid it's pretty wet."

He raked an unholy gaze over her. "Wet's okay with me."

After he'd disappeared out the door, Madison paced the empty hut. Why was she so edgy? So itchy? So...*what?* What was she feeling? Why was she so attracted to a guy she didn't even know? It was beyond all logic, and Madison was nothing if not logical. What was this unexpected chemistry between herself and Strickland? And most importantly of all, why was she letting it get to her?

Whenever she looked at him her mind just went haywire and all she could do was imagine him naked. Her heart would start hammering and her nipples would harden and she was terrified she was going to set off the stupid chastity belt. Then she'd have to fend off Bianca or Emma or Izzy asking what was going on.

In despair she stared out the window at the driving rain

and wondered just how long they were going to be stuck here. If it didn't stop raining soon Madison was very afraid she'd find herself falling for another ne'er-do-well.

"YOU HUNGRY?" Jake asked, toweling his hair dry.

"Starved. What did you bring with you?"

"Protein bars, trail mix, bananas and a handful of muffins from the breakfast buffet. You?"

"I've got string cheese, turkey jerky and dehydrated soup mix. Big package of peanuts, peanut-butter crackers and two apples."

"We've got the makings of a hellacious picnic." Jake plunked down on the floor of the hut.

Madison sat down beside him. They went through their backpacks and came up with the food, spreading it out before them. "So," she began, stripping the peel of a banana. "I told you about my ne'er-do-wells. What's your story? You married?"

He raised his left hand, bare of any rings. "Footloose and fancy free."

She hadn't thought he was married, but she wanted it confirmed. Not that she really cared. "Ever been married?"

"Not even close."

"How old are you?" She munched on the banana.

"Twenty-nine."

"Peter Pan complex?"

"Naw, just not all that impressed with the institution of marriage."

"You come from a broken home, too?"

"Fractured is more like it. I never knew my dad. My mom…well, let's just say she's a real peach. She married a guy who didn't want children, so she left me with my grandmother, who died shortly after I went to live with her. That's when I learned the joys of the foster-care system."

Sympathy tugged at her heart. "Oh, Jake. How old were you?"

"Seven."

"Poor kid." She had an urge to reach out and hug him, and Madison was not the huggy kind.

He pulled a mournful face. "It's tough being me."

"I wasn't making fun."

"I know. I was."

"I can't imagine what that must have been like for you. And here I was whining because I had a Jack-in-the-box dad who showed up when I least expected it."

"Hey, don't feel sorry for me. I ran away when I was twelve, and I met this really cool guy, Joe Maxwell. He took me in, gave me a job washing dishes in his bar and grill, treated me as if I were his son."

"Joe sounds wonderful."

"He is." Jake nodded.

"So what about school?"

"Not so great at academics, but I shone on the track field."

"I bet you were popular with the girls."

He looked surprised. "How did you guess?"

"With that face? Come on."

"You think I'm handsome?"

"I think you're a man who damn-well knows the effect he has on the opposite sex."

"So you admit I affect you," he said with satisfaction, nibbling on a handful of trail mix.

Madison couldn't stop her gaze from watching the column of his throat move when he swallowed, couldn't stop her eyes from sliding down to where the *V* of his shirt revealed a sexy sprinkling of chest hairs. "Hell no," she lied through her teeth.

"Whew." He dragged a hand across his forehead, wiping off imaginary sweat.

"Whew? You're relieved I'm not attracted to you?"

"Yeah."

"Why's that?" she asked, knowing she shouldn't, but her old insecurities were welling up. When it came to men she was so inept. Falling for the wrong ones, not falling for the right ones. It was best if she just stayed away. Honestly, strapping on this chastity belt was the best thing she'd ever done. It was a great reminder to keep her head screwed on straight.

"Because if you were as attracted to me as I am attracted to you we'd spontaneously combust."

Oh, dammit, why had he said that? And why was he staring at her as if she was the most fascinating woman on the face of the earth?

"You're a ne'er-do-well in nerds' clothing," she scoffed. "And I have to ask myself why?"

"That's where you're wrong," he said.

"What about?"

He cocked an eyebrow, blatantly eyeing her lips and drawled, "There's a lot of things I do very well."

Don't fall for it. Don't you dare fall for it. Seriously, stop looking at him. Stop thinking about him. Calm down. Cool down.

Just then her satellite phone rang. She had to dig to the bottom of her backpack for it.

"Madison? It's Izzy, are you okay?"

"Sure," Madison said. "Why wouldn't I be okay?"

"Well, you're heart rate is galloping like a thoroughbred on Derby day and you're breathing heavily. Are you over-exerting yourself in the jungle?"

Madison glanced over at Jake who cracked one of those "do-me darlin'" grins of his, and she quickly looked away. "We...um...I got lost."

"Hey, your temperature just went up half a degree. Are you sure you're okay?"

"I'm fine."

"You sound weird. Did guerillas take you hostage?"

"Costa Rica is perfectly safe."

"Why is your voice...omigosh, you're with a guy!"

"I'm in a stressful situation, Izzy. I really don't have time for a phone call."

"Is he cute? Your vital signs are telling me he's cute."

"I'm going to have to hang up now."

"So you're out of the bet?"

"No, I'm not out of the bet."

"But you're not going to have sex with this guy."

"Of course not."

"But you want to."

"I do not!"

"I beg to differ. Your body says otherwise."

"The damned underwear must be faulty. I fell down a ravine and got muddy and showered with it on and apparently something short-circuited."

"Yeah, your libido." Izzy hooted. "And here everyone thought you were the one who was going to win."

"How do I know you're not cheating?" Madison countered.

"My sensor hasn't gone off."

"Why is that, by the way?"

"I've been a good girl."

"Either that or you had your electronic guru friend Hunter tamper with the sensor and you've been blissfully having sex while the rest of us suffer."

"Ooh, you get cranky when you're not getting any." Izzy laughed.

Madison notched her chin upward. "I *am* going to win."

"Not unless you get your vital signs down."

"Fine." Madison took a calming breath. "Is that better?"

"Nope."

She could feel the heat of Jake's gaze on her but she refused to look up at him. "I've got it under control."

"You sure about that?"

"Absolutely."

"All right, but if you sleep with him—"

"I'm not sleeping with him!" she snapped and closed her eyes and let out a soft groan. He'd heard that.

"I believe you. Or I will when your vitals go down."

"They'll go down. Give me five minutes."

"I'm calling you back if they're not."

"Fine."

"And if I have to call you back and you don't answer…"

"I know, I know, I'm out of the competition." Madison hung up the phone without even saying goodbye. Sometimes Izzy could get on her last nerve. Good thing she loved her friend like a sister. She stuffed the phone back in her bag and kept taking long, slow deep breaths.

"What was that all about?" Jake asked.

"Long story."

"We got time. And no place to go."

What the hell. She might as well tell him. He'd already seen the chastity belt. "My friends and I have a bet going."

"Let me guess, it has something to do with that contraption you're wearing."

"Yeah," she admitted.

"Is this like that episode of *Seinfeld* where Jerry and George and Kramer and Elaine all vow not to, um…have any kind of sexual contact?"

"It's exactly like that."

"Better you than me." Jake shook his head.

"Are you saying you have no self-control?"

"Depends. How much is the bet?"

"Five hundred dollars."

"No way. It would take a lot more cash to keep me from pursuing a woman I was interested in."

"How much?"

He shrugged. "I dunno."

"Put a price on it. How much would it take to keep you celibate?"

"With a woman like you?" His grin turned downright sinful. "Million and a half."

"Why the half?"

"Taxes."

Madison laughed. She didn't even know why. But the way Jake was looking at her made her feel desired in a way she'd never felt before.

"Listen, I have to get my pulse rate down or I'm going to be out of the bet."

"You want me to go outside?"

"No, just stop staring at me and talk about something boring."

"Boring, huh?"

"Really boring. Your last dental appointment might work."

"That would cool off anyone," he said. "I had two cavities the last time."

"Sweet tooth?"

"You got it." He winked and she felt a blush heat her

cheeks. Dammit. She'd never get her pulse under control at this rate.

"All right, that's not working. I need to calm down. There's been too much excitement for one day."

"Wanna try yoga?"

"You know yoga?"

"Sure."

"Okay, what do I need to do?"

"Breathe from deep in your diaphragm." He placed a palm on his belly and inhaled deeply.

Madison followed suit and quickly felt her body relax. It was working.

"Close your eyes."

She did.

"Put your index fingers to your thumbs."

She did that, as well.

"Now, just keep breathing like that."

In a few minutes a gentle peace had settled over her. Crisis averted. She opened her eyes, found Jake's eyes on her. "What are you looking at?"

"You've got a little bit of banana right there." He touched his own face just above his upper lip.

"Where?" She rubbed her face with her fingers.

"Missed it."

She swiped her whole palm over her mouth. "How about now?"

"Still there."

She scrubbed her face. "That get it?"

"No." He leaned in toward her and softly brushed his index finger over the spot. His touch sent tingles racing through her body.

Their gazes locked. He was so close to her she could feel the heat of his breath on her skin. Goose bumps carpeted her arms. They stared into each other. The calmness evaporated.

Madison couldn't say who made the first move. She thought it was him, but it certainly could have been her. Most likely it was both of them simultaneously riding the wave of attraction and going for it, but the next thing she knew, Jake's mouth was on hers and hers was on his and her wet hair was tumbling to her shoulders and his hot arms were encircling her and they were kissing like there was no tomorrow.

JAKE sure as hell hadn't meant to kiss her. He'd been trying not to the entire day. One minute he was telling himself, *Don't kiss her, don't you dare kiss her,* and the next minute he had her in a lip-lock so startlingly delicious he forgot to breathe. All he could do was inhale.

Maddie, he thought. *Maddie, Maddie, Maddie.*

He tightened his arms around her waist and she linked her arms around his neck and they were on the ground, Maddie's soft breasts mashed beneath his hard chest muscles. She tasted like peach nectar, thick and sweet and heavenly. He kissed her as if his very life depended on it. Kissed and kissed and kissed *and...*

Then her damned cell phone rang.

Her friend again, he had no doubt, calling to jump on her for engaging in sexual activity.

Well, not quite sexual. Not yet.

The boner he was sporting might refute that. Instantly, Jake broke off the kiss and rolled off her, his head spinning. Somewhere along the way he'd unbuttoned Maddie's jeans. Hell, he didn't even remember doing that. What was happening to him? He felt shaky and breathless.

This is crazy. You can't be falling for her. No way, no

how. Wrong time, wrong place, wrong woman, wrong everything.

And yet, one look into her eyes and he was helpless. She could ask him whatever she wanted and he would give it to her.

This was crazy. Nonsensical. And he didn't like it one bit.

Maddie was on the phone, assuring her friend she was not having sex. That wasn't a total lie, but they'd been rushing headlong toward it.

He got up, paced to the door, shoved a hand through his hair and stared out at the downpour. Good grief, they were trapped here until it stopped raining. He scanned the sky, which seemed to be growing darker and wetter with each passing moment, and tried to ignore the ache in his rock-hard penis. He could smell Maddie on his skin, taste her on his lips. She was an amazing woman.

If they weren't in Costa Rica and she wasn't a conservationist and he wasn't an orchid smuggler, well… But he *was* an orchid smuggler, and she was a conservationist, and even beyond that was the whole footloose and fancy-free motto that defined him. He wasn't changing for any woman, even one as compelling as this one. Even though whenever he looked at her he felt something click inside him as if for the first time everything was right with the world.

"You okay?" Maddie asked, coming up behind him.

Jake blinked, glancing over his shoulder at her. Clearly she was off the phone. "I'm fine."

"You don't look fine."

"Well, I am," he lied.

She squared her shoulders. "I'm fine, too."

"Good."

"Great."

"You out of the bet?" He nodded at the phone.

"Not yet."

"Haven't quite crossed the line?"

"No," she said, "and I'm not going to."

"That's good. You probably really need that five hundred dollars."

"Not as much as I need my sanity."

They looked at each other and he could see in her eyes she was as unnerved as he was. He blew out his breath, then said what he'd dreaded telling her. "It looks like we're going to be stuck here all night."

$$\underline{4}$$

IT RAINED for three solid days.

Madison checked in with Professor Hampton and learned the rest of the group had never left camp because of the inclement weather. Dammit, why hadn't she checked the forecast? She and Jake were out here all alone.

To keep their hands off each other, they'd spent the time talking about their childhoods, their pasts, their likes and dislikes. They'd played twenty questions and truth or dare, and when they tired of that they resorted to the childhood game, I spy.

I spy with my little eye something very sexy, Madison thought as she looked at Jake.

She told him about orchids, why she loved them, why she'd spent her life collecting them—moth orchids and lady's slippers and vanda and cattleya and Burana Sunshine. Jake spun stories about the places he'd been. South America, South Africa, Australia, Europe, the Orient.

They discovered they had much more in common than they would have ever suspected, given their divergent backgrounds—Madison was working on her PhD and Jake had gotten a GED instead of finishing high school. She was scientific and analytical while he trusted his gut and acted on instinct. She liked time to think things through, he was fast-paced and action-oriented. But, they both loved roller coasters and in-line skating. Both of them were night owls, preferring to sleep in and stay up late. They agreed that while it was noble to be politically active, neither of them had ever bothered to vote. Their favorite comfort food was macaroni and cheese—the kind that came in a box. They preferred the same brand of beer, chose corn chips over potato chips, and thought kettle corn was just plain weird. They learned that they shared an obsession with reality TV and they enjoyed old B monster movies. They'd each been to the International Spy Museum in Washington D.C. on several occasions and realized to their surprise that on one occasion they'd both been there on the same day.

By the time the rain stopped on the third day it was as if they'd known each other their entire lives.

They woke from their sleeping bags to the sound of birds chirping and sun flooding in through the boards of the hut. Jake yawned and stretched as Madison put on her glasses and finger-combed her hair.

"Ten o'clock," she said, strapping on her watch, and yawned. "How late did we stay up last night?"

Jake shrugged. "I'm not one for keeping to a schedule, but I think it was pretty late. I was having a lot of fun trying to guess where your birthmark is."

Madison rolled her eyes. She should never have told him about the heart-shaped birthmark. When she'd refused to show it to him, he'd started trying to guess where it was. Teasingly whispering, "Breasts? Belly? Thigh? Tushy?"

That little game had heated her up quick as his gaze had caressed every body part he called out. But it'd ended when Izzy phoned her to declare, "Either do him or don't, Madison. This foreplay business is going on too long and it's rude to keep waking me up in the middle of the night."

Remembering, she raised her head, saw Jake giving her the once-over. Was he remembering, too? A hot rush of sensation passed through her and she quickly ducked her head.

"You're a beauty, Maddie, even if you don't know it," he said.

Where had that come from? Madison caught his gaze and cleared her throat. She wasn't accustomed to men complimenting her for her looks. For her expertise, yes. For her intelligence, sometimes. Brainy girls, she'd discovered, intimidated most guys. Even the brainy guys, because they were afraid of the competition.

But not Jake. Jake seemed genuinely impressed with her.

"Better get a move on," she said. "Today might just be the day we find the amore."

The muddy traipse through the jungle quickly grew hot, sweaty and tiresome, and they were down to their last canteen of water. Madison kept checking the map and her coordinates. They were so near the amore, she could taste it.

But when they reached the area where she was certain the flowers would be—where the soil nutrients and the rain levels and the amount of sunshine was absolutely perfect for orchid growing—there was nothing but more jungle fronds and tall dark trees and mud, mud, mud.

Disappointment swept through her like a snowstorm dusting across the plains. Hampton had been right and she'd been wrong. "Dammit," she muttered, startled to realize she was very near tears. Madison didn't cry. It took a lot to make her weep. But she'd been so sure...so certain that this was it. She'd been passionate about orchids for most of her life, and the amore in particular had captured her imagination. What was she going to do about her dissertation now?

She only had one option. Go back to Hampton with her tail between her legs and beg his forgiveness.

"What's wrong?" Jake asked.

She shook her head. "This is where the amore was supposed to be. I was convinced."

Jake scratched his head. Had he bet on the wrong pony? Had he let his attraction to Madison sway his decision to throw in his lot with her instead of sticking with Professor Hampton? Yeah, probably.

But oddly enough, he didn't really care. Yes, he still wanted to save Joe's Bar and Grill, but these last few days with Madison had been among the best in his life. Even if they hadn't had sex. Maybe precisely because they hadn't had sex. He'd gotten to really know her before sleeping with her. Sort of a first for him. He couldn't regret having spent time with her. Even if that meant he'd lost out on his chance of getting his hands on those orchids.

In fact, being with her, hearing her talk about the importance of orchid conservation, listening to the pure passion in her voice when she spoke of the beautiful flowers, brought home the message that his goal was corrupt. Stealing and smuggling orchids wasn't the way to save Joe's place. He got that now. Before being enlightened by Madison, he'd been very cavalier and he was ashamed of himself.

Now, all he wanted to do was help her find the orchids. Not for him, but for her.

He watched her shoulders sag and her eyes mist as she fought back tears and Jake felt something inside him shift, change. She had worked and strived and struggled for years to get here and it was slipping from her grasp. Jake didn't really understand what that was all about. He'd never put that much effort into anything. He skated by, having fun, following his whims, doing as he wished. His fear of deprivation and his need to keep himself entertained had prevented him from searching for deeper meaning.

In her, he saw the value of slowing down and taking his time, of being deeply invested in something. Of doing more than skimming the surface before flitting off to something new. He was always on the look-out for adventure, always chasing the next thrill. He'd believed staying busy, focusing on happy things was the key to navigating life's bumps and potholes. For him, stealing the orchid had been about more than looking out for Joe. It was a challenge, a caper, a great big game just to see if he could go for it.

But Madison had made him realize something extremely profound, and to Jake, who was not prone to profound thoughts, it was an earth-shattering insight. As long as he was in a tunnel-visioned pursuit of happiness and satisfaction, he would never obtain it. Fulfillment was not the result of anticipating the next adventure waiting around the corner. It was based on appreciating what you had in the moment.

And right now, he had Madison.

"I've been kidding myself." She groaned.

"Now I wouldn't have expected that from you."

"Expected what?"

"Self-pity."

"I'm not feeling sorry for myself." She paused. "Okay, yes, yes, I am. I've spent three years searching for this orchid only to be foiled again. I think a little self-pity is allowed."

"C'mon," he said, taking her hand. "We're not giving up yet. Let's keep looking."

"It'll be getting dark soon. We need to make camp for the night."

"Just a little longer," he coaxed.

"All right," she grumbled. "But it's no use."

"What's it gonna hurt?"

She shrugged and followed where he led.

They pushed through the heavy vegetation, fighting the plants thwarting their progress. Their backpacks might as well have been lead weights. Jake's shoulders ached, his calves ached, hell, everything ached. They scaled a small rise and walked through a tunnel of trees where the setting sunlight flickered in long yellow rays as they entered a small clearing.

Madison suddenly pulled back on his hand. "Jake," she whispered. "Look."

WHAT MADISON saw stole all the air from her lungs. She stood there, mouth agape, heart thumping, mind spinning, senses buzzing.

For there, growing on the surrounding trees, were hundreds of amore orchids stretched out before them, comets of deep midnight blue tangled up among the jungle vines. Madison had seen many orchids in her life, but none like these. They possessed enormous long stems and delicate petals that resembled female sex organs.

A slow smile spread across her face and her eyes narrowed in delight. Here lay paradise.

"Damn," Jake said. "Will you look at that?"

Simultaneously, they breathed in, inhaling the incredible fragrance of orchid. It was a merry-go-round of smells—a rose-like scent combined with jasmine, rye bread, musk, wintergreen, cinnamon, cloves. The odd but enticing chemical combination sent a rush of heat through her nose and into her lungs, warming her blood, sending red-hot waves of desire radiating straight to the tingling spot between her legs.

Amore orchids.

She twirled in a circle, arms outstretched, dizzy, happy. This then was the scent of love.

The smell was immediate and undiluted. It needed no words to translate. It smelled like sex.

Madison caught her breath, spun around. Jake was watching her with heavy-lidded eyes and she knew he felt it, too. This urging, the yearning to be joined.

The look he gave her said, *I can turn your insides into chocolate pudding,* and the cocky tilt to his head left her airless and addled. A deadly combo. This smell. That man.

There was no nerd here. No matter what he pretended, this man was a rebel through and through. A good-time bad boy who wasn't good for her. Another ne'er-do-well. And she knew he was going to lead her into temptation and beyond.

His eyes danced with naughtiness and when he dropped his backpack, she dropped hers, too. Then he slowly stripped off his black T-shirt, and when she got a good look at his honed, muscled chest, her heart slammed into her ribcage, a car wreck of chaotic sensation.

"C'mere," he murmured in a husky, dusky voice as ripe as the orchid scent. His expression said he knew her right down to the depths of her soul.

Jake held out his hand.

In a dreamlike state, she moved toward him, pulled by a force she didn't understand but could not resist.

Languidly, he removed her glasses and tucked them into his backpack for safekeeping. He dug around for a condom and when he found it he held it up like a great prize.

He stalked back to her, slipped his arms around her, tugging her down onto the grass in the clearing, kissing her tenderly as if she was as rare and precious as the orchids.

They finished undressing each other. Shoes flying, pants

sliding, chastity belt unlocking, until they were totally naked before each other.

Madison's cell phone rang, the sound echoing in the forest.

"Your friends," he said.

She crawled across the grass, fumbling for the phone in her backpack. She answered it by gasping, "I'm out."

"Wh—" Bianca's voice said on the other end, but Madison never heard the rest because Jake took the phone from her, tossed it over his shoulder and pulled her down again.

He kissed her hard and long and hot. They lay on the slick, wet grass, the sleepy sun filtering through the tree branches. All around them the orchids, heavy and sweet, glowed in that dying light. Under his deft fingers, her aching body bloomed, as spectacular as the flowering plants, and she shivered against his rousing touch.

Lust swamped her. She had to have him. Had to have him or she would surely die. She pulled his bottom lip up between her teeth and he made a noise of pure enjoyment.

He cupped her face in his palms, dipped his head and kissed her with a soul-stealing, grade-A, world-class kiss that curled Madison's toes. The moment was brilliant. He was brilliant. It was her most brilliant fantasy come to life.

She burrowed into him, her breasts pressed flush against his muscled chest. He ran his palms up and down her arms. She threw back her head and he tracked kisses over the tender areas of her throat, nestling and nibbling.

Experimentally, he rubbed his thumbs over her nipples and they beaded up tight. "Ah," he said. "So you like that?"

"Uh-huh." A hazy hotness draped over her, thick with

sexual urgency. She wanted him so badly she couldn't speak.

"What about this?" He laved his tongue along her collarbone.

She shuddered against him.

"And this?" Lightly, he stroked circles on the inside of her arm.

"Beast," she gasped.

"Exactly." He grinned.

The force of his desire caused her to tremble and sweat. Her knees quivered. Her heart pounded.

He tunneled his fingers through her hair. She felt his presence in every cell of her body.

He loved her with his mouth, tonguing her with amazing tenderness, a slow glide from the sensitive spot behind her knee, around to her kneecap and up her inner thigh until she was rolling in ecstasy.

She floated, body-less. She was total awareness, her entire being a giant throb of sexual energy.

He kissed lazy circles of heat and she was transfixed. Finally he edged to the spot where she wanted him to be, at the sweet V between her legs.

His wet tongue teased, slowly licking her outer lips. Inhaled her. Then caressed her with the sensuous sweep of his tongue.

He sucked at every fold, lapped at her ridges and lifted her buttocks to devour his meal. An electric flash of brilliant energy lit the inside of her head and all the air was drained from her lungs.

She surfed his tongue, owned it. She hovered on the brink of orgasm but he would not let her fall over. A steady strumming vibration began deep in her throat, emerging as a wild moan.

She thrust herself against his mouth, gripping the sides of his head with her thighs, letting her juices flow.

He released her but didn't remove his tongue from her twitching clit. His tongue danced with it, wriggling nimbly.

Her skin was incredibly sensitive, her body tingling and tender. She tried to push him away, it was simply too much pleasure, but he stayed put, pushing his tongue deep inside her. Then out and down to the region beyond.

This new sensation drove her into a frenzy. Her muscles flexed. Blinding flashes of light. A rushing sound like ocean waves in her head. Uncontrollable spasms rattled her body.

Her world quaked.

His fingers touched and tickled and tingled. Her butt, her inner thigh, her clit. He slid one finger deep inside her wetness, while his tongue continued to strum the feminine head of her.

She didn't know where she was or who she was with. Who was she? Woman or creature?

His hands were broad and warm. His mouth an instrument of exquisite torture. Time spun, morphed, as elusive as space.

She was spellbound, mesmerized, entranced. Embraced by a longing so precious and severe she couldn't breathe. In delicious anguish, she cried out her delight.

He rocked back on his heels, clasped her to his chest and held her tight, hands threaded in her hair, until her crazy thudding heart calmed.

Then when she had rested, he made love to her again, sinking his flesh into hers. He wanted her as desperately as she wanted him, with the same high-octane intensity.

As their bodies joined and hotly fused in the moonlight—at some point the sun had gone down and the moon had appeared—orchid pollen travelled on the air, floating on the night breeze. The petals rustled, their minute fluttering as primal as the heavy breathing Madison and Jake shared.

Scent drenched the air—orchids and mating—combining, fusing, part of an ancient dance as old as the sun and the moon and the stars.

The entire time he was buried inside her, he stared into her eyes, as if he was lost in her gaze and could not find his way out. Did not even want to find his way out.

Two became one.

A single being.

Trembling and clinging.

His cock filled her up, pushing far inside her until he could go no farther.

Then he pulled back. In and out, he moved in a even tempo that rocked her soul. He rode her and she rode him until they both came in a blazing, blinding light.

AWHILE LATER, Jake awoke and listened to Maddie's soft breathing. Her head was resting on his chest and it felt so good he smiled into the darkness.

And then he remembered why he was in Costa Rica in the first place.

He had a secret to confess to her. Something he should have told her before he made love to her, but he'd been so caught up in the moment, so under her spell, so excited for her over the discovery of the amore orchids that he'd followed his instincts and not his head.

Like always.

Except everything else was different here and his usual behavior no longer applied. Not with Maddie. With her he wouldn't have to look for adventure or scout out the next thrill. She was the adventure, being with her the thrill. He just prayed she'd forgive him when he told her the truth.

"Jake?" she whispered into the sultry darkness.

"Uh-huh."

"Do you have any more condoms?"

"Yes."

She walked her fingers up his chest. "Could we um… go again?"

Now's the time, speak!

He was going to. He intended to, but then she was touching her hot, sweet tongue to his nipple, and all conscious thought flew right out of his brain. He searched for the condom, found it, got it on somehow, then rolled over, taking her with him, cradling Madison in his arms.

She let out a soft little moan and opened her legs.

He held his weight on his forearms and slid into her welcoming wetness. Overhead, the moon shone down on her face. He stared into her bright, trusting eyes and moved his body over hers, fitting perfectly against the curved hollow of her hips.

Maddie caressed his face with her tender hands, murmured endearments in a lyrical tone. But soon the hushed whispers turned to gritty groans and heated gasps. She made him feel like the best lover on earth.

He loved hearing her sexy sounds. In fact, he was pretty sure he could listen to them for the rest of his life and die a happy, happy man.

And when her release came, he twined their hands together above her head and rocked into her with one fierce thrust. She arched her back, eager to meet him, and wrapped her legs around his waist, pulling him in as deep as he could go. Their fingers were locked, their gazes welded as they came in one shattering shudder.

"Wow," she breathed a few minutes after they'd come spiraling down. "Just, wow."

"That doesn't begin to cover it." They were lying on their backs, their eyes directed up at the vast field of stars, wrapped in a cocoon of amore-orchid scent.

"That was the best ever," she whispered.

"For me, too," he confessed.

"It was…you were…you make me feel so…"

He waited for her to finish, wondering how he made her feel, when the steady sounds of her breathing told him she'd fallen asleep. He smiled. He'd worn her out.

He marveled at how he could be so connected to someone he'd only known for four days. It made no sense, but he couldn't deny it.

Could he be…was he possibly…falling in love?

5

MADISON woke just after dawn. Jake lay next to her, snoring lightly. She propped herself up on one elbow and stared down at him. His tousled hair curled across his forehead. In repose his firm jaw seemed softer. The man was fricking gorgeous. How had she managed to snag a guy like him?

You didn't snag him. This was just a fantasy come true for one night. Don't read any more into it than that.

It sounded good as a theory but she greedily wanted more.

Be real. You're working on your doctorate. You live in New York. And he...

Suddenly she realized she didn't even know what he did for a living. He'd told her about his extensive travel. That he worked for various companies, but when she'd pressed for details, he had glibly changed the subject in that smooth way of his.

Uneasiness skittered over her. Another ne'er-do-well. Boy, could she pick 'em or what?

Well, he'd distracted her long enough, she had an orchid to catalogue. Where were her glasses? Oh, yeah, he'd put them in his backpack. She eased to her feet, gathered up her clothes, hurriedly dressed, and then went to retrieve her spectacles.

She dug around on top and didn't see them. She pushed aside his change of clothes, the last of their food supplies and that's when she found it.

The six-inch harvesting knife. A pair of stainless-steel scissors. A bottle of root stimulator and an instruction book on how to transplant and transport orchids.

Her blood ran icy. She stared at the items, praying she wasn't seeing what she was seeing. Hoping there was a perfectly innocent explanation for why he was toting these things around with him, but knowing in her heart of hearts there wasn't.

"Maddie."

She spun around, the treacherous items in her hands.

Jake was on his feet, standing naked, completely exposed, a guilty expression on his face. "I can explain."

Madison felt sick to her stomach. "We never dreamed someone would be low enough to use our expedition. Follow us, yes, but to hire a soldier of fortune to masquerade as a conservationist and then betray us… It all makes sense now. The nerd disguise—which by the way was pretty transparent. The way you flit from country to country, how you never would explain what it was you really did for a living."

She had to give him credit for looking totally miserable.

"You're an orchid thief. A smuggler."

He raised a finger. "Small point, I'm not an orchid thief or a smuggler. At least not yet. I came here to become one, yes, but mostly I'm just a jack-of-all-trades for hire."

"Mercenary," she spat out.

He nodded. "Yeah, I've been called that, too."

She threw her head back and yelled at the sky. "I can't

believe this is happening to me again. This one is the ne'er-do-well to end all ne'er-do-wells. What is it?" She threw out her arms. "Am I a ne'er-do-well magnet?"

He grabbed his jeans and jammed his legs into them. "Maddie, you gotta listen to me. I did have bad intentions when I initially came on this trip, but after meeting you, getting to know you and the way you love those flowers… I've never seen anyone as passionate about anything as you are about those things. So I changed my mind. I wasn't going to steal your precious orchids."

"How could you even consider doing it in the first place?" She sank her hands on her hips. "It's illegal."

"I wasn't doing it for me. I needed the money to help Joe keep his bar and grill."

"You expect me to believe that cock-and-bull story?"

"I can't control what you believe, but it's the truth." He came toward her, reached out a hand. "I realize now that it's wrong and I'm sorry."

"Oh, do not touch me. Don't you dare touch me."

"Last night was—"

"A huge mistake. Huge." She was so angry that she couldn't begin to express it. "You used me."

"Only at first, once I got to know you, things changed."

The pain in her heart was so acute she could barely catch her breath. She'd been hurt before, but she'd never felt as utterly betrayed as she did right now.

"This looks really bad, I know, but we can get past this. I can change. I want to change. You make me want to be a better man. Madison, please—"

She cut him off. "You don't care about these precious orchids, and you don't care about me. You're a thief and a smuggler and I can only assume a liar, as well."

He deserved it. Jake understood that. But it killed him that she thought he'd intentionally set out to hurt her.

"I can't believe I lost my chastity bet over the likes of you," she said.

The anger in her eyes tore at his heart. She hated him. Madison wasn't interested in hearing a single word he had to say.

He felt as if he were shrinking, growing smaller every second, losing any self-respect he might have possessed. His loosey-goosey values had led him here. He'd allowed his need for fun and excitement and adventure and the thrill of the chase, to override his common sense. Sure, he'd done it to raise money for Joe, but there were other ways to get money. If he was being honest with himself he'd admit he'd accepted the job from Liu for the challenge. Madison was right. He was all the things she'd called him. A soldier of fortune, a thief, a smuggler, a mercenary and a liar.

"I want you to pack up your things and leave this instant," she said, her voice as cold as an arctic breeze. She pointed in the direction of base camp. "If you go now, I won't tell the authorities you were here. It's a better deal than you deserve."

"I can't leave you in the jungle alone," he protested.

"She's not alone," a male voice said from behind them.

Jake spun around to see Professor Hampton, Bunk, Lucinda and all the other volunteers glaring at him as if he was scum of the earth.

"She might not turn you over to the authorities," Hampton said. "But I sure as hell will."

SINCE Jake hadn't actually stolen the orchids or tried to smuggle them, the authorities couldn't really hold him, although they indicated he was no longer welcome in Costa

Rica. As a show of good will, he gave them Liu's name as a collector to watch out for. Now he could add ratfink to his long list of sins.

With a heavy heart, he flew home to L.A.

He'd brought this on himself. He'd been glib and cavalier. He'd taken life too lightly. He hadn't considered the consequences of his actions.

But he was sure considering them now. He'd been so close to something truly wonderful and, by being deceptive, he'd let it all slip through his fingers. It was a wake-up call. He thought of the amore orchid, almost the color of Madison's hair. Dark and soulful. Growing deep in the jungle. A rare and unique beauty nearly impossible to find.

Once he was on American soil, Jake called Mr. Liu and told him not only was the deal off, but that the amore orchid was probably going on the endangered species list soon.

Liu cursed both in English and Taiwanese, threw around empty threats. Jake didn't care. He had bigger fish to fry. Like helping Joe keep his bar and grill. And coming up with a plan to win Madison back, although deep inside he feared he was beyond redemption in her eyes.

Jake arrived at Joe's place feeling lighter just from having told off Liu. He hadn't warned Joe that he was coming home and he was surprised to see the bar and grill closed. What was going on? He turned to climb back on his Harley when Joe came around the side of the building whistling happily.

"Jake!" Joe exclaimed, and his eyes lit up. He clasped him in a warm embrace. "When did you get back?"

"Just now."

"Why didn't you call me?"

Jake shrugged. "I guess I was too embarrassed."

"Embarrassed about what?"

"Can we go inside and talk?" Jake drank in the sight of the man who was the only family he'd ever known. Stocky, balding, but still in good shape for a man his age. He had a lot of years left in him.

Joe shook his head. "She's not mine anymore."

"The bank foreclosed?"

"Nope, I sold her."

"Joe!"

"Don't look so distraught, Jake. It's just a building."

"The bar and grill is your life. You've been in business for twenty-five years."

"And tied down 24/7 for twenty-five years."

"But…but…I thought you loved the place."

"I do. Did. It got old, though. Especially once you were grown up. I kept her for as long as I did because you enjoyed coming back here from your adventures. But when the economy turned and customers started staying home to drink beer and barbecue in their backyard, it was a sign for me. I'm not getting any younger, kid, and if I want to have a few adventures of my own before I die, I realized the time is now."

Here he'd been thinking losing the business was going to break Joe's heart, but he seemed happier than Jake had ever seen him. "But you were so upset when you told me you were going to have to sell."

"I'm not saying it didn't hurt. Growth always hurts. But you can't move forward until you let go of the past. I'm ready to step into a bright new future. What about you?"

Jake told him then. About Liu and the amore orchid. About Madison. About the mess he'd made in Costa Rica. When he was finished, a smile tipped the corners of Joe's lips. "This funny to you, Joe?"

"Not funny." Joe's eyes danced with amusement. "Inevitable."

"Inevitable that my recklessness would lead me to trouble?"

"Inevitable that you would fall in love."

"Nah…" Jake shook his head. "Yeah?" He nodded. "You think?"

"Only one thing could make you take a hard look at your life and reevaluate it to this degree. And when you talk about her, your entire face lights up. Buddy boy, you're stone cold in love."

MADISON had always assumed that finding the amore orchid would be the greatest moment of her life.

It wasn't.

She took no joy in it because for some cursed reason all she could think about was Jake. Yes, he'd duped her. Yes, he'd had bad intentions. But he hadn't stolen the orchids.

That's because you caught him before he had a chance.

She remembered the way he'd looked in the jungle, standing before her completely bare and vulnerable, begging her forgiveness, and a lump of despair scaled her throat. She believed him. Believed he'd recognized that he'd made a mistake, admitted it and was truly remorseful. But she'd been so hurt that she hadn't been able to get past her own pain and offer him the forgiveness he had clearly wanted.

She'd been back from her trip for two weeks, teaching the second half of the summer-school session for Hampton. He was still in Costa Rica, soaking up the glory for having discovered the amore, barely giving her any credit at all beyond mumbling to the press that her calculations about soil-nitrogen levels in that region led him to the area. What had she expected from a raging egomaniac?

Men. She was sick of the lot of them.

"Hey, Ms. Garrett," one of the male students said, yanking her distracted thoughts back to the present.

She blinked at the small group of summer-school students seated before her. "Yes?"

"I heard on the news this morning that a Taiwanese billionaire was charged with hiring orchid smugglers to steal rare orchids from around the world."

"Oh? I hadn't heard that."

"What do you think about the practice of orchid-smuggling? Honestly, what's the big deal? I mean come on, it's just a flower. It's not like it's drugs or anything."

Madison launched into a lecture on why the illegal trafficking of orchids was detrimental on so many levels, but in the back of her mind she kept considering what the student had said.

When the class was over, she dismissed the students and bent to collect her things to get out of the way for the next class. She heard footsteps in the auditorium, but she figured it was just a student coming back for something they'd forgotten. Until a deep masculine voice said, "How you doin', Maddie?"

She whirled around, her heart suddenly pounding. When she saw Jake standing there looking deadly handsome and uncharacteristically serious, she felt her grip loosen on the books and papers in her hand, felt them tumble to the floor. She stood frozen, unable to move to pick them up, pinned to the spot by Jake's wistful gaze.

"What are you doing here?" she asked sharply.

"I came to see you." He sauntered toward her.

"Well, I don't want to see you. I thought I made that clear enough in Costa Rica."

"You did." He nodded, coming up onto the lectern with her. "But I can't stay away. I know I hurt you and I'm more sorry than words can ever say. I hope you'll give me a chance to make it up to you."

"Why should I?" she demanded, crossing her arms over her chest in a desperate bid to protect her melting heart.

"I've already made a start."

"You turned Liu in."

"Yes. Someone taught me the importance of protecting the orchids. I understand now how inconsiderate I've been. She also taught me something else." With his eyes holding hers, he reached out to take her hand, interlacing their fingers.

"What's that?" she whispered, wanting so badly to believe him.

"I'm never going to find joy gallivanting around jungles."

"No?"

"Joy comes from the heart, Maddie. And my heart is here."

Her pulse leapt. "What are you saying, Jake?"

"These kinds of feelings don't come along every day, and I think we owe it to ourselves to see where it might lead."

"I'm sorry, but I promised myself I was never going to get involved with any more ne'er-do-wells. And poaching is a big deal to me."

"Then you're in luck."

"Oh?"

"From now on, I'm going to be an always-do-well. I'm doing my best to make amends and I hope you'll give me a chance to prove it to you."

"You're going to change, just like that?"

"I'm going to try. I've taken a regular job."

"Doing what?"

"Eco-tourism. I'll be working for a company based here in New York that sends out experienced guides to lead conservation-minded individuals interested in doing their part in preserving endangered species. Can you find it in your heart to forgive me?"

"You're really going to do that?"

"Maddie, I'd do anything to redeem myself in your eyes. You've shown me the error of my ways and I'm praying you won't walk away from what we could have because of my mistakes."

"I guess there's no sense in being a hard-ass," she whispered, wanting so much to forgive him. "I think I can give you another chance."

Relief crossed his face, immediately replaced by the impish grin she knew so well. "Hey, I need a hard-ass to make me toe the line, but from what I remember, your fanny is not too hard, not too soft, but just right." He reached out to splay a palm to her backside. "You keep me on my toes, Madison Garrett, and it's one of the things I love most about you. I need someone like you in my life."

"And you keep me from being too much of a pointy-headed intellectual."

"Who knew," he murmured, lowering his head to steal a kiss, "that the daring adventurer and the calculating professor would turn out to be the perfect match?"

"Who knew?" she echoed and kissed him back.

"Now about that heart-shaped birthmark you teased me with…. It was too dark in the jungle for me to find it that night we made love. Are you ever going to show it to me in the light of day?"

She glanced toward the door, saw they were alone, then coyly raised her shirt and inched down the waistband of her pants to reveal the birthmark.

"I spy with my little eye something very, very sweet."

Then Maddie took him back to her apartment, showed him her bedroom postered with photographs of the amore orchid she'd taken in Costa Rica and there with the smell of passion in the air, they made love all night long.

And then there were two.

NO TURNING BACK

1

Emma comes face to face with the one that got away....

"YOU'VE BROUGHT ME to the ends of the earth to die," Emma Jacobs accused her best friend Izzy Montgomery.

"Ends of the earth? What are you talking about?" Izzy said. "It's just Colorado."

Emma—who was a city girl through and through—stared at the vast expanse of trees and sky and land and water. No taxis honking. No smell of hot-dog carts. No crowds jostling. No smog. No hot asphalt. Nothing to remind her of home.

"Come on," Izzy urged. "Stretch your wings. Try something different. Don't be afraid to expand your horizons. That's what I was telling Hunter before we left New York. His girlfriend broke up with him."

"I've been in the wilderness before," Emma grumbled. "Had a couple of bad experiences there. I went to summer camp when I was a kid and it was awful." She'd been stung by angry bees and broken her arm falling off a ledge during a hike. "Speaking of awful, I'm sorry to hear that about Hunter. He's a nice guy. One of the few."

"He's better off without her. She kept complaining about the amount of time he spent at my apartment. She couldn't get it through her head that Hunter and I are just friends."

"Well, I understand where he's at right now—that just-broken-up hell. I'm still hurting over Ryan," Emma said.

"Hey, you told me you wanted to go somewhere you'd forget all about Ryan. Well, there'll be no sign of him here."

Ryan Andrews. The guy she'd met on a Bahamas cruise last year. The same guy who'd broken things off with her because he'd found someone he liked better. Emma gritted her teeth. Izzy was right. Okay, so this place was a god-forsaken wilderness, but there was absolutely no chance of running into metrosexual Ryan in these rugged parts.

"You're thinking about Ryan," Izzy said.

"How did you know?"

"You've got this expression on your face like you've been eating lemons."

Emma blew out her breath. "I'm totally over him," she said. "I view him as a necessary speed bump on my road to stop romanticizing every relationship the way I've done since…"

Well since Trent Colton. She thought of how he'd looked at eighteen, cocking a deadly grin and leaning in to steal a kiss from her in the hallway of her high school in Terry-town, New York. There were some things a girl never forgot. Her first kiss, her first love, the first man she'd ever slept with. Trent had been all three. Emma gulped, feeling her cheeks color as she remembered her youthful mistake. It had all started with Trent—her tendency to romanticize love. If she could go back in time, she'd do a lot of things differently.

"C'mon," Izzy said, slinging her backpack over her shoulder. "Let's get registered."

Izzy started for the small log cabin situated at the end of the road where the bus had dumped the group, joining the four other women headed in the same direction. This particular tour was advertised as women-only. The point was to get out in the wilderness, hike some mountains, raft some white water and learn a few survival skills.

When Izzy had first posed the trip while Madison and Bianca were off jetting the world and falling in love, Emma had been all for it. She'd needed something to take her mind off the fact that as a librarian she didn't possess the funds for flying off to Brazil or Costa Rica. Plus, she'd wanted to get as far away from the opposite sex as she could. But now that she was here, she wasn't so sure. Where were the comfy hotels? The spas? The room service?

"Ah," Izzy said, taking a deep breath and then expelling it. "Smell that crisp, pine-scented air? It's a good twenty degrees cooler here than in Manhattan."

It was, but that wasn't a selling point. Emma liked heat. As soon as the temperature dipped into the sixties, she hauled out sweaters and jackets.

"At least we're not going to have to worry about the bet while we're out here," Izzy remarked, slowing down so Emma could catch up with her. "No hunky guys around to distract us from our goal."

"Which is?" Emma asked, mincing carefully around a collection of rocks that had fallen from the rise onto the path.

"To become stronger women."

"Oh, yeah, that goal."

"Did you wear your special lingerie?" Izzy asked.

"Of course I did," Emma replied, shifting her mental focus to the lingerie she had on underneath her jeans and T-shirt. "Madison and Bianca are monitoring us. But shh, please don't call it that in public."

"I'm going to win, you know," Izzy said smugly.

"Not likely. I don't jump into bed with guys the way you do."

"Ouch, the kitten's got claws."

"Okay, sorry, that sounded mean, but come on, Izzy, you have been with a lot of guys."

"Which is why I'm sure I'm going to win the bet."

"I'm not following you. If you have trouble controlling your libido—"

"You're the one who has issues. You fall in love with every guy you sleep with."

Guilty as charged. She'd slept with three guys in her twenty-seven years and she'd fallen in love with all three of them. Trent hardest of all.

"I know that I can go without sex, but I don't know if you can go without falling in love."

"Don't be ridiculous."

"We'll see," Izzy said. "May the best woman win." With that, she opened the door to the log cabin and stood aside for Emma to go in first.

The other four women who'd been on the bus with them were chattering like bees in a hive. Excited, intense. In contrast, Emma was depressed, a bee without wings. She was not looking forward to this vacation. She'd just wanted out of the city, away from places she'd visited with Ryan.

"Hi!" greeted a cheery woman in her mid-thirties. She had short dark hair and a perky way of bouncing on her toes. "I'm Selena. I just got divorced and I'm ready for the next chapter in my life. How 'bout you?"

"I'm Emma, I just got out of a relationship, too."

"Married?" Selena asked.

"No."

"You dodged a bullet. Stay single."

"Um...thanks for the advice."

Besides Selena there were Deanna and Jessica, traveling companions from Ohio. They shared a house in Cincinnati and loved taking active vacations together. They'd been wanting to take a white-water rafting trip for years and they were "so enthused to be here." Emma guessed them to be in their late thirties, early forties. And there was Myrtle, sixtyish, slim. She was recently widowed and her daughter had bought the trip for her. Myrtle's mood seemed to match Emma's. Unsure about the whole thing.

Behind the desk, a young woman Emma estimated to be about five years younger than her, was checking people in. The girl was vaguely familiar, but Emma couldn't place her. As she and Izzy waited their turn to sign in, a truck rumbled to a stop outside the door. Emma didn't pay much attention. She was wriggling around, trying to get the lingerie unbunched from around her waist without being obvious about it. The cabin door opened. Emma tugged. The women in the place let out a collective sigh. Emma shifted her backpack and finally glanced up.

All the air left her lungs.

A man stood in the entrance of the place that was supposed to be for women only. A tall, dark, ruggedly handsome man in scuffed hiking boots and a battered straw cowboy hat looking for all the world as though he'd stepped from the set of an Old West movie.

Emma's stomach lurched. Not just because he cut a powerfully sexy image, but because she'd know that face anywhere. Had dreamed of it many a night. Her shoulders tensed. Her thighs tingled. Her hands curled into fists.

Trent Colton in the flesh, looking a hundred times sexier than he had been ten years ago.

Izzy nudged her in the ribs. "See, I told you I was going to win the bet."

"You set me up," Emma hissed.

Izzy shrugged, grinned.

"But…" Emma darted another glance at Trent. He was busy studying a clipboard and hadn't seen her yet. "How did you find him?" she whispered.

"Remember that night we went out to Club Sizzle?"

"The week after Bianca went to Brazil and Madison headed to Costa Rica?"

"Yeah, and you got a little tipsy and started gushing to me about your first love?"

"No."

"Well, you did. Anyway I looked him up on Facebook and voilà, I discovered he ran a wilderness-vacation-adventures outfit. That's when I proposed the trip."

"How did you know he was the right Trent Colton?"

"There weren't that many, plus he was in your age group and you listed the same high school. I took a shot."

"What if he's married? I mean if you lured me here thinking I'll rekindle the relationship and you'll win the bet, then you had to find out his marital status."

"It said 'single' on his Facebook page."

Oh gosh, oh gosh, oh gosh. It was Trent and he was single. Emma's heart pounded so loudly she feared everyone in the place could hear it. Particularly Trent.

She gulped. Every muscle in her body urged her to sprint from the cabin and run after the bus headed back to Durango, but it was too late. Like it or not, she was stranded here.

"Hello, ladies," Trent greeted the group. "I'm Trent Colton, your guide for this adventure."

Izzy made yummy noises—so did Myrtle.

Deanna and Jessica looked as though they didn't care either way.

Selena scowled. "A man? Why are we stuck with a man? I thought this was supposed to be a women-only trip. I came out here to get away from men."

Amen to that, Emma thought.

Trent raised his palms. "I'm sorry to disappoint you, ma'am, but we're short-staffed for the summer. My name's listed as the tour guide on the website. My sister Angie will be happy to refund your money and arrange transportation to the airport if my gender is an issue for anyone."

Ah, that explained why Angie was familiar. When Emma and Trent had been dating, Angie had been thirteen. She'd changed a lot, grown into her looks.

"Why can't Angie guide us?" asked the disgruntled woman.

Angie rounded a hand over her belly. "Sorry, I'm six months pregnant."

A sympathetic murmur went up from the group.

"My brother knows what he's doing. You're in good hands," Angie assured them. "He's a true professional."

"I want my money back," Selena said. "Please arrange for my shuttle to the airport."

Here's your chance. Take your money and hop on the bus out of here with Selena.

Emma stepped forward, but then something stopped her from saying anything. Running away wasn't the answer. If she really did want to make a clean start for the future, she'd have to face the past. And the past was standing right across the room from her.

"Personally," Izzy whispered. "Even though I know he's

yours, I don't mind enjoying the scenery for the next seven days."

"He's not mine," Emma snapped. "Not anymore."

"Emma?"

At the sound of Trent's voice pouring over her, smooth as honey, Emma closed her eyes. He'd finally seen her. No running away now.

"Emma Jacobs, is that you?"

Emma suppressed a groan and turned to greet him.

"Or are you going by another name now?" Trent asked, weaving toward her.

Emma shoved a hand through her hair. It was hard to smile when she felt so shaky inside. "No, still Jacobs."

"How did that happen?" Trent asked, raking an appreciative gaze over her body. "I would have bet even money that someone would have snatched you up and put a big diamond ring on your finger by now."

"Nope, no snatching."

Trent tipped back his cowboy hat, tilted his head, grinned. "His loss is my gain."

Just as knee-wobblingly charming as ever. Emma's heart was thumping madly now.

They stood looking at each other, and it was as if she was eighteen again and madly in love for the first time. All the bittersweet, angst-filled teenage emotions she thought she'd forgotten all about came surging to the forefront, and for a split second, she could not get her breath.

"Well…" he said, his eyes eating her up. "Well, you sure look good."

Emma's cheeks heated. "Um…so do you."

"We need to catch up."

"Um…yes…let's do that."

He waved his hand at the counter. "I'll let you get

registered, then come on out to the landing where we're outfitting everyone with their gear.

"Okay," she replied, not knowing what else to say.

Trent went around the desk and through a door behind his sister. The minute he disappeared from sight, Emma's shoulders sagged. "I can't do this, Izzy."

"Scared you're on the way to losing the bet?"

"No, terrified I'll make the same mistakes I made ten years ago."

"You're tough. You can resist him."

"Bringing me here is like putting chocolate cake in front of someone who's been on a low-carb diet for a year."

"Yep."

"And you're not the least bit remorseful."

"Nope."

"If you weren't my best friend I'd call you something that rhymes with witch."

Izzy was impervious. "Hey, do what you gotta do."

"Witch."

"Hopeless romantic."

"Heartless love 'em and leave 'em."

"Sticks and stones."

"You owe me big-time."

"All right, I'll grant you that. I promise to do your laundry for a week when we get home."

"No way. You're taking me out to eat somewhere really expensive."

"Okay. I'll have that fifteen hundred dollars from you guys after you all lose the bet to me," Izzy chuckled. "I can swing that."

"I'm not losing the bet." Emma gritted her teeth. This wasn't about the bet at all. This was about her past and the way she'd fallen into the same tender trap. Picking men who looked like Trent. Both Ryan and her college boyfriend,

Doug, had possessed the same dark hair, tall stature and
rugged attractiveness as Trent. Apparently, he'd gotten into
her blood and, as much as she believed she'd put the past
behind her, one glance at him was enough to prove her
completely wrong.

Once Izzy had signed them in, Angie gave her a list of
do's and don'ts for successful white-water rafting, then
instructions on where to pick up their gear and directions
to the launching dock. Deciding that she was going to
view this as a positive and let go of her anger and anxiety,
Emma followed Izzy to the lockers where they could store
their purses and luggage and pick up sleeping bags and
backpacks.

Once they were outside again, the sheer beauty of the
place bowled her over. The river stretched out to their left.
She could see glimpses of it through the trees. Myrtle,
Deanna and Jessica had already picked up their packs and
had started walking down a narrow path to the dock where
Trent Colton stood surveying everyone like the captain of
his domain. Which, she supposed, he was.

He grinned and waved at Emma.

Stupidly, she grinned and waved back. What in the heck
was wrong with her? She couldn't rewrite the past. How
had she gotten here?

Oh yeah, Izzy. Her friend could think again if she
thought she was going to win that bet. Emma was strong.
She was resolute. She was not going to cave simply because
the one-who-got-away was strutting around on the dock
like a runway model.

Stop watching him!

Ah, but she couldn't. He moved with such agile grace,
she was mesmerized. Compelled by a force beyond her
control, caught in a whirlpool of emotions, all she could
do was stare.

No, no that was wrong-headed thinking. This was not beyond her control. She was here on vacation. She planned on learning how to raft white water and start a campfire and all that other good survivalist nonsense. She was just going to forget that Trent had once held her in the protective circle of his arms, that she had once rested her head on his shoulder and dreamed of being Mrs. Emma Colton. That was the stuff of fairy tales. Romantic and unattainable. A fantasy.

And this was her chance to stomp it out once and for all.

2

She was sexier than ever.

Lust, hot and hard, grabbed Trent in a death grip as he watched her come down the hill toward the dock.

He stared at her feet and raked his gaze up to that pretty face that still occasionally haunted his dreams. Trent swore under his breath. At twenty-eight Emma was in the prime of her youth. She wasn't even dressed sexily, but to him, she would have rocked a potato sack with those luscious curves. She had her wheat-colored hair pulled back in a ponytail, topped off with a pink baseball cap. She wore a matching pink T-shirt that nipped in at the waist to show off her body, a pair of faded jeans and brand-new hiking boots. Blisters were in her future.

The sweat trickling between his shoulder blades had nothing to do with the warm weather and everything to do with the gorgeous blast from his past. He ran the back of his hand across his brow and blew out a pent-up breath. Why was she here? Had she known this was his outfit when she'd signed up? Or was it just an interesting coincidence?

She struggled with her bag. It was forty pounds and she looked as if she didn't weigh much more than a hundred herself. It was all he could do to keep from rushing over to help her. But the point of this retreat was to help women find their inner strength. The concept had been his mother's brainchild when she'd been forced to find her own power after his father's death. A year ago, after he'd sold his start-up company specializing in eco-friendly outdoor wear to a big corporation for several million dollars and Mom had a new love in her life, she'd turned over the reins of Wild West Adventure Tours to him.

Trent shook his head. He still couldn't believe Emma was here on his river.

Emma Jacobs.

The girl he'd lost his virginity to the summer after his senior year in high school. She'd been pretty then, but now her beauty was striking.

But he didn't have a second to sort out his feelings, because here she was, pink-cheeked and slightly out-of-breath from exertion.

He couldn't resist the temptation any longer and reached to take the pack she lugged with both hands. "Here, let me get that for you."

She held on to it. "That's okay, thanks, I've got it."

They stood on either side of the backpack, their hands just inches apart, their eyes engaged. Her full, kissable lips were glossed with a sweet shade of pink and her blue eyes were disarmingly wide. Her fragrance tangled up in his senses—she smelled like yellow roses in full bloom. Trent clenched his jaw against the sudden surge of lust rushing pell-mell through his blood stream.

The passing of a decade hadn't done a damn thing to quell his desire for her.

He was so absorbed in staring at her he barely noticed the other guests piling up at the dock waiting for instructions. *Snap out of it.* He pulled his gaze from Emma's face and started doing his job.

Once everyone had taken their places, it was only him and Emma left standing at the launch site. "You might want to take off your clothes," he said.

Her eyes widened. "What?"

"I mean," he said, feeling like ten kinds of fool. "Jeans and a T-shirt aren't the best materials to wear rafting. You need fleece or synthetics that whisk water away and keep you dry." He tugged on the material of his pants. "Like these. Didn't you read our brochure?"

"Obviously not. I didn't bring anything close to that."

"My sister Angie has some loaner fleece you can borrow."

"Okay," she said. "I'll be right back."

"Hurry," he urged. We're suppose to leave promptly at ten."

Five minutes later she returned, this time dressed appropriately. She climbed down into the raft where they were all waiting for her. Trent tilted his head for a clandestine view of her behind. Damn, but she had a fine ass.

Completely thrown off his game, Trent forced his attention to the business at hand, clambering into the rear of the raft and going through the launch preparations. Five minutes later, they were on the river. The beginning of the trip was a leisurely drift and he took the opportunity to give the usual safety briefing followed by a spiel about the geography of the river, the flora and fauna and what was coming up over the course of the next week. They would go ashore at dusk at a campsite where Angie and her husband David had left tents and food. The guests would set up their own tents, start a fire and cook their own meals. Trent would be on hand if they required help.

The summer sun was already hot, but the river was cool. It was sourced from mountain run-off, so it never really got warm. The air was clean and crisp. Not a cloud in the sky. Trent's kind of morning. He loved the outdoors. He loved what he did for a living. Loved working with his sister and her husband. Enjoyed people. He'd been born for this life.

He watched Emma, who was sitting in the front of the raft beside Myrtle. The older woman was regaling her with stories about her grandchildren. Emma turned her head to look over her shoulder at him as she paddled and their eyes met. He felt it again, that heat, the chemistry that time had not erased. If anything, the attraction was more potent. The wind tousled her ponytail and he noticed there were three small opals nestled in each of her earlobes. She shouldn't have been sexy wearing the bulky yellow life jacket, but she was. When the tip of her pink tongue flicked out to moisten her lips, his body grew hard.

She lowered her lids and her long, light-brown lashes cast a whispery shadow on her smooth, sun-burnished cheeks. Then she shifted her gaze again. Her blue-green eyes were the color of a cool mountain pool. No, he took that back. Her eyes put mountain pools to shame. Even from this distance, he could smell her scent. It hadn't changed in ten years—yellow roses tinged with a hint of green apple.

Finally, she glanced away. Feeling edgy, he focused on paddling the boat with the big oar and steering them down the river.

He remembered Emma as being amazingly feminine, not the outdoorsy type at all. But here she was embarking on a wilderness rafting trip. It was nothing he would ever have expected of the teenaged Emma. His admiration for her went up.

What was she searching for? Most of the people who came on the "women-only" trips were in the process of reinventing their lives. Newly divorced or widowed, or just ready to push themselves out of their comfort zones. It was rewarding to see them come away from this experience transformed. What was Emma seeking to overcome?

The rest of the morning passed pleasantly. They had a couple of days before hitting the real white water and he used the time to teach his passengers about how to navigate the waves. They went ashore mid-afternoon for a simple lunch of fruit and sandwiches and to stretch their legs.

Emma went off by herself and perched on a large, flat rock underneath a shady oak tree, while the other women went wading. He noticed she had a book with her and he had to smile. This was the Emma he remembered. His little bookworm.

He scaled the rock to sit beside her. "So."

"So," she answered back.

An intimidating silence stretched between them. Her skin looked baby-soft, as if she pampered it nightly with creams and lotions. He ached to stroke his fingers over it.

"What are you reading?"

She held up the cover for him to see. *The Adventures of Huckleberry Finn.* "I thought it was fitting, given the river setting."

Another awkward silence.

"How are your parents?" he asked.

"Good. How are yours?"

Getting conversation out of her was like getting water from a stone. "My dad died a few years back," he explained. "Aneurysm. One minute he was here, the next minute he was gone."

Sympathy pinched her features. "Oh, Trent. I'm sorry to hear that. I always liked your dad."

"Do you remember what he used to call you?"

"Peanut," she said, "because I was so small."

"He underestimated you."

Emma raised her head. "He wasn't the only one."

"What brought you on a rafting trip with your friend?" He gestured toward the water where Emma's gregarious friend was laughing with the other rafters.

Emma shrugged. "Vacation."

"That's it?"

"I needed a change."

"From what?"

She met his eyes. "Men."

"Romance gone bad?"

"That really isn't any of your business."

"Here I've gone and made you mad."

"I'm not mad, I just don't want to talk about it."

"He hurt you that much, huh?"

"Not as much as you did." She snapped her mouth shut as if she'd said far more than she wanted to.

The awkward silence returned. Trent couldn't stop himself from staring at her. The woman always had mesmerized him with her wavy wheat-colored hair and those large blue-green eyes that seemed to see the best in people. She'd once seen the best in him and then he'd gone and blown it all. He cleared his throat, swallowed, uncertain of what he should say next. Having her on the trip was unnerving and unexpected and he was unsure how to proceed. "Did you come on this trip to reconnect with me?"

"Don't flatter yourself. I didn't even know you worked here. Izzy made all our travel arrangements."

"Maybe it's fate, us meeting again like this."

"Naw, it was Izzy trying to win a bet."

"Excuse me?"

She waved a hand. "It's a long story. Short version: Izzy was trying to play matchmaker and she set me up."

He cocked his head. "Why did you stay?"

"Huh?"

"You could have left. Used the excuse that I wasn't a female guide on your women-only tour and gotten your money refunded."

Emma shrugged, lifting one slender shoulder. "I guess when I saw you I realized a lot of the mistakes I'd made with men could be traced right back to you. Maybe I'm supposed to face my past in order to move beyond it."

He didn't care for the sound of that. He didn't want her moving beyond him.

She was trying to appear nonchalant, reabsorbed in her book, but unless he missed his guess, she was far more aware of him than she wanted him to know. "I'm on this trip to forget about a guy," she said. "If you're wondering."

"I was," he admitted.

"So I'm not looking for romance. In fact, I'm looking for the opposite of romance. I spent way too many years searching for my knight in shining armor. It's taken me ten years to realize there's no such thing and that fairy tales don't come true."

"What are you saying? That you don't believe in love?"

"Love? Maybe. But I no longer believe it's all about hearts and rainbows and slow dances and flowers and chocolates and long walks along the beach holding hands. That's stuff for greeting cards, not real life."

Honestly, he agreed with her. Reality was a lot messier—and much more fun—than a silly picture on a greeting card.

"So what about you?" she asked.

"What about me?"

"You ever been married?"

He shook his head.

"Why not?"

"Came close once, does that count?"

"Close only counts in horseshoes. What happened?"

"It wasn't any one thing. Just a lot of little missteps."

"Maybe you need to face your past, too," she whispered.

A feeling grabbed hold of Trent. A feeling he couldn't deny or ignore. A possessive sensation that defied all logic, but it was there nonetheless. Taking them both totally by surprise, he leaned over, cupped her face between his palms and kissed her the way he'd been wanting to kiss her since he'd seen her standing in the office.

"Oh." She breathed in the word, parting her lips, letting his tongue slip deep inside the sweet, hot recesses of her mouth and glide lazily over her tongue. Desire raged inside him, fierce and demanding—all from a simple kiss.

He could only remember the incredible sensation of slipping his cock into her tender folds, her legs thrown over his shoulders, his fingers threaded through her hair and his hungry mouth at her nipples.

Trent barely suppressed the groan of lust rising in his throat. He imagined how tight she'd feel closed around him, so hot and wet. His testicles drew up tight at the thought.

Without even trying, this woman could still bring him to his knees.

STUNNED, Emma sucked in a deep breath of air, amazed, embarrassed, exhilarated. Huckleberry Finn dropped from her hand. Omigod. Trent was kissing her. On a rock by the river, in nowhere, Colorado. Trent. Her first love. The man she hadn't seen in ten years. It was surreal.

So what was she supposed to do now?

Ignoring it was out of the question. This wasn't an innocent kiss. No friendly peck for old times' sake. This kiss meant business. And Emma was completely unprepared

for it. Her heart skipped a beat, did a somersault, landed
upside down and skipped another beat.

Disoriented, Emma raised a palm and splayed it against
his chest, meaning to push him away. She could feel his
heartbeat through the material of his all-weather garment,
absorbed the radiating heat of his masculine flesh. He was
warm and alive and solid against her hand. She recognized
that he was tense, his chest muscles hard and strong from
hours of rowing on the river.

And he was still kissing her.

Emma tried to tell him to stop, but the only thing that
escaped her lips was a soft whimper of air that sounded
more like a plea than a protest.

Suddenly, Trent let her go.

She gulped, blinked and gingerly lifted a finger to trace
her feverish lips. Her body had gone all melty and wet and
she would have slipped right off that boulder and tumbled
headlong into the river below if he hadn't draped his thigh
over her legs. Hemming her in against a rock and a very
hard place. He made her feel small and vulnerable and that
was scary.

One look in his eyes and she was burned to a crisp. Her
blood was pumping on pure adrenaline.

Dear God, she thought, what did that kiss mean?

IT TOOK all the strength Emma had to stay cool around
Trent. Every time she glanced at him her heart lurched
drunkenly.

The man still affected her and his kiss proved it. Even
after ten years. He'd been the template for all the relationships that had followed as she'd chosen one wrong guy after
another. Well, she was breaking the pattern, shattering the
mold. Izzy had actually done her a favor, tricking her into

this trip. It was the perfect way to face her past and finally let it go.

That all sounded so good, so rational, so sensible.

She didn't feel that way at all. Their eyes would meet and the old spark ignited, stronger than ever, and good, rational and sensible went up in flames of lust. Why hadn't the chemistry died after all these years? Why was there still a spark?

Doesn't matter if there's a forest fire, you're not acting on it. Trent Colton is bad news. Always has been, always will be.

How many tears had she cried into her pillow over him? Far too many to count.

Emma stuck her oar in the water and concentrated on pulling her load. Even though she hit the gym three times a week, her upper body was not prepared for this strenuous workout. After half a day on the river her arms were aching and her shoulder muscles burned. Grimly, she bit down on her bottom lip, determined to soldier through. She might not be an outdoorsy type, but she tried to look strong.

She turned her head, attempting to take in the beauty of the place—the conifers, the fat blue jays chattering along the banks, the cool sounds of water rushing over stone.

The sound of water rushing over stone?

"We're coming to our first set of rapids," Trent confirmed. "They're light. Between a Grade I and a Grade II. Nothing to worry about. It's a good way to get your feet wet, so to speak."

The other women in the raft made excited noises. Emma said nothing because fear churned her stomach. The rapids sounded pretty loud to her.

They rounded the bend and her pulse quickened as she got her first look at the water slipping rapidly over big slabs of dark, smooth rocks. Uh-oh. She'd been dreading this part every since Izzy had proposed the trip. From behind her, she heard Izzy shout, "Woo-hoo!"

Emma tightened her grip on the oar and clenched her jaw.

"Here we go!" Trent sang out.

The raft bounced over a couple of rocks, the water spraying up to splash their faces. It was cold, but that was nice on the hot day. The air smelled clean and crisp. After a few little skipping bumps, Emma's heart was pumping blood fast, roaring in her ears, and she was sure her sexy lingerie was going off, but it didn't matter. Izzy was with her and knew she was not having sex. She had a good excuse.

Speaking of her wild and crazy friend, Izzy was on her feet, arms raised over her head, head thrown back like a hedonistic goddess, yodeling her thrill at the top of her lungs. Envy slithered over Emma. She wished she could be as spontaneous as Izzy. A little reckless, a little nutty, fully living instead of always reading about it in a book.

Hey, you're here now. You just shot the same rapids that she did.

And yet it seemed that Izzy was having a lot more fun.

Determined to have a good time, Emma tried to imitate Izzy, raising her arms and yelling as loudly as her friend. But her oar snagged on a rock and hung there. Emma jerked, whipping the raft in that direction. Trent was hollering at her, but she didn't understand what he was saying.

"Ooh, ooh," Emma exclaimed.

Physics was not her friend. For one thing, she'd barely passed it in high school. For another, it grabbed hold of her and yanked her into the water. One minute she was hooraying herself and the next minute her butt was bumping along the rocks.

She spiraled. She whirled. She opened her mouth to

scream and took in water. Panic closed over her. She kicked, thrashed.

Something clutched at her back and she felt herself being lifted free from the water. That's when she realized Trent had a vise-grip on her collar with one hand, his other hand grasping the waistband of her pants. His rough knuckles grazed her lower back. Good thing she was five-foot-nothing and didn't weigh much. Otherwise he probably couldn't have hauled her soaking-wet ass into the raft again.

There were other hands now, the other women tugging her into the raft. She lay there on the bottom, staring up at the sky, gasping, feeling like a total fool. How come Izzy could twist and shout and act all wild and crazy and make it look cool, but when she tried it...*disaster.*

Face it, you're just not the wild and crazy type.

Leave that to Izzy. And to Trent, who used to be the wildest boy she knew, which of course had been part of the attraction.

Speaking of Trent, he was leaning over her, concern furrowing his brow. His fingers snapped off the strap anchoring her helmet to her head and he slipped it off.

"Emma?" He sounded rather far away. "Emma, speak to me. Are you all right?"

It was the same sensation she'd had the day Ryan told her it was over and she'd downed half a bottle of chardonnay in three, long inhaling swallows. Her head was muzzy, stuffed with wool. "Uh-huh."

"How many fingers am I holding up?"

She frowned, stared, tried to concentrate. "Three."

Relief crossed his face. "Can you sit up?"

"Sure." She tried to sit up, but dizziness assailed her and she had to lie back down. "Okay, maybe a little slower this time."

Trent placed his hand to the base of her head, cradling

it in his palm. It felt so good. That hand. So strong and steady. Slowly, he helped ease her to a sitting position.

Emma blinked and glanced around, noticing that the raft had drifted to the shoreline during her little madcap adventure. "I'm fine."

"I want you to sit here in the rear of the boat with me," Trent said. "No more paddling for you for the rest of the day."

"That's not fair to the others," she said.

"We're almost to the campsite. Don't worry, you can make it up to them by cooking dinner. You do know how to cook, don't you?"

"If by cook you mean calling for takeout, then yes, yes, I do."

"I'll help," he said.

"You don't have to coddle me." The last thing she wanted was a cozy scene making dinner with Trent. How could she resist him if she was doing something as intimate as cooking dinner with him? "I'll get Izzy to help."

"I'll hold you to it," he said, then addressed the others. "Let's get paddling, everyone."

3

TRENT ROWED at the stern of the raft, guiding the boat and its passengers safely over the river. His heart was still in his throat over Emma going into the water. Rafting could be quite dangerous. Something he didn't know if she fully appreciated, but for the moment, she was behaving herself, sitting quietly beside him.

Her exuberant behavior had been so unexpected. When he'd known her before, she'd been the quintessential good girl to his bad boy, which he supposed was part of the attraction. Now, however, he saw she'd changed. She was more daring than she used to be. More expressive, as well. He liked this spunky side to her, had always suspected it existed.

She sighed and shifted in the boat, rotating her right shoulder.

"You all right?" he asked.

"Stop mother-henning me," she said. "You can't show me favoritism over the others."

"It's not favoritism. I would be concerned about any of my passengers who fell in the water. You might have hit your head, and even with the helmet on you could have suffered an injury."

"I'm fine, stop fretting. In fact, give me an oar, I want to paddle."

"Too late," he said and nodded with his head to a stretch of flat, grassy land on the shoreline to their right. "We're at the campsite."

They docked the raft and climbed out. Emma was the last to go ashore. Trent held out his hand to steady her, but she shook him off. "I can do it."

Sure, he got the message loud and clear. Hands off.

Angie and David had driven in the supplies, but rather than just leave them as they normally would have, they were waiting with concern written all over their faces.

"What's up?" Trent asked.

"We've got some bad news from home for Deanna Price. We waited so we could drive her back to the office."

Deanna's face paled and her friend Jessica put an arm around her shoulder. "What's happened?"

"The Cincinnati police called. Your fifteen-year-old son has been arrested for stealing a car and going joyriding."

"Where was his father?" Deanna asked. "He was supposed to be with his father."

Angie shook her head. "I wasn't given more information than what I just relayed to you."

"We'll cut the trip short," Jessica soothed Deanna. "Our kids come first."

"This is terrible, just terrible," Deanna wrung her hands.

"Don't worry about a thing," David assured her. "We'll gather up your things for you and drive you into Durango tonight."

Everyone gathered around Deanna, offering her encouragement and support as she and Jessica climbed into David's SUV.

"Do you remember when we got arrested?" Trent whispered to Emma.

"How could I forget? It was the beginning of the end for us," she said.

Before Trent could answer, Izzy wandered over. "Too bad for Deanna and Jessica, huh?"

"Too bad," Emma echoed.

"Our tour group is dropping like flies." Izzy rubbed her palms together. "First Selena, then Deanna and Jessica. I'm starving. When do we eat?"

"When I get it cooked," Emma said.

The guests weren't pampered on this tour. It was up to them to set up their tents, start a fire and prepare the food. His job as a guide was simply to oversee, give advice and help out if things didn't go according to plan. Emma falling into the river, for instance. But the purpose of the trip was to encourage independence and strong self-esteem.

Trent watched Emma trudge over to where the camp stove and food supplies had been set out. She rubbed her shoulders, clearly uncomfortable. She wasn't used to rowing and he imagined her muscles were cussing her out pretty good right now. Izzy and Myrtle went to set up the tents while Trent secured the raft and the equipment.

But the news about Deanna's young son was fresh in his mind. It was true what Emma had said. Their arrest had been the beginning of the end of their relationship. But clearly not the end of his feelings for her.

"How HARD could this be, right?" Emma looked at Izzy.

"You're asking me? My microwave and I are very friendly for a reason."

"Well, I have to make amends for falling into the river and causing everyone else problems. Dinner has to be good."

"Define good."

"Edible."

"Oh, we can do edible." Izzy opened one of the big cardboard boxes containing the food supplies and started pulling stuff out. "Powdered eggs—better save those for breakfast. Cans of tuna. Do you know how to make tuna casserole?"

"I think you need an oven for that."

"Ah, canned chili. This is a piece of cake, just dump it in a pan and heat."

"Got any cheese in there?"

"Sadly, no. Apparently we're not on the gourmet-food rafting tour."

"Chili it is," Emma said, then set about trying to figure out how the stove worked.

To her surprise and pleasure, she quickly had the stove up and running and the chili heating. Izzy had found a box of crackers to accompany the dish.

If Emma's shoulders hadn't been burning like fire from all the paddling and the bumping against rocks when she'd fallen in the river, things would be going well for a change.

Izzy had wandered off, as Izzy tended to do. She couldn't sit still for long. Emma had often wondered how she got her comic strip drawn and written in time to meet her deadlines.

Trent sauntered over. "How's it going?"

"Fine." Emma shrugged her shoulders, trying to work out the kinks.

"Rough day."

"Yeah, well, you know. I've had worse."

"Your shoulders are killing you."

"How'd you guess?"

"You've been rubbing them and shrugging ever since we hit shore."

Trent came around behind her and laid his hands on her shoulders. Instantly, she tensed. His body heat radiated from his fingertips into her skin. She was aware of everything. The closeness of his body, the smell of his skin, the cool breeze blowing in with twilight.

Gently, he began massaging her sore muscles. It felt so good, a small, helpless moan escaped her lips.

"You should take an anti-inflammatory," he said. "There's ibuprofen in the first-aid kit."

"You think I'm a wuss, don't you?"

He chuckled. "Not in the least."

"Then why are you laughing at me?"

"I'm not laughing at you. I'm amazed at how much you've changed. The old Emma wouldn't even go on a camping trip, much less row a boat over the rapids or cook dinner on a camp stove."

"It wasn't that I wouldn't," Emma said. "I was just too scared to try."

"How come you're not scared now?"

"I've learned that life is a lot more fun when you take a few chances," Emma murmured, purring like a cat as his fingers hit the right spot. "Seriously, you could give up this guide gig and become a masseur. People would pay big bucks for those magic fingers."

His fingers found a knot in her shoulder muscles and he used his knuckles to dig in.

"Ow, ow, don't stop."

"Does it hurt?"

"Yes, but in a very good way." She didn't realize how seductive the words sounded until they were out of her mouth. Or how dangerous it was to let him massage her neck and shoulders. Already sparks of awareness were lighting up through her body. One small spark and she was ready to catch fire.

He kept massaging circles into her skin. "You know," he began, "I don't think I ever apologized for getting you arrested."

"Water under the bridge," she said.

"I hated that you got caught up in it."

"I survived."

"Yeah," he said. "But we didn't."

"Um…" She stepped away. "That'll do. Thanks. Thanks so much."

"Your muscles still stiff?"

"I'll live."

He dropped his hands, stepped back. "I'll leave you to it."

"Thanks," she repeated.

Trent turned and walked away. Emma's shoulders sagged and she let out a breath. How in the world was she going to last the rest of the trip with this man? The only thing she had going for her was that they were not alone in the wilderness. Otherwise, she had no doubt she'd be making the same mistakes she always made. Romanticizing something that should not be romanticized.

And before she could stop herself, her mind was off, spinning fantasies of what could have been, or what could still be.

WHILE Emma had been cooking, Izzy had set up their tent. Emma had just enough energy to slide in, zip it up and lie down to sleep. As they lay there listening to the sounds of the night—insects chirping, small animals rustling the leaves, the snores from fellow campers—Izzy suddenly asked. "So what happened with you and Trent? Why did you guys break up?"

"We just weren't compatible."

"You look pretty good together to me. In what ways are you not compatible?"

"He's an outdoor guy and I'm just not that into bugs and spiders and snakes and sleeping on the ground. Plus in high school, I was college-bound and he wasn't. We had different priorities, we were just too different in general."

"Maybe so, but whenever he sees you his whole face lights up."

"It doesn't." Emma paused to consider Izzy's observation and touched her cheeks with her fingertips. "Does it?"

"Yep."

"Well, there's the fact that I'm something of an introvert and he loves people."

"You love people."

"Yes, but only one at a time."

"So what was the straw that broke the camel's back? Why did you break up?"

"He got me into trouble and my parents forbade me to go out with him."

Izzy sat up. "He got you pregnant!"

"Shh, not that kind of trouble."

"Then what?"

Emma didn't like to talk about her secret shame, but maybe if she told Izzy she'd quit pestering her. "He got me arrested."

"What? You? Miss Goody Two-Shoes?"

"I'm not that good."

"Well, you're certainly not bad. You don't even keep overdue library books."

"Of course not, I'm a librarian."

"So what'd you do? Steal a car and go joyriding like Deanna's kid? Shoplift?"

"We graffitied a water tower. Or rather, Trent graffitied it. I was just along for the ride."

"Cool. What did you write?"

Emma paused, remembering that night. She'd sneaked from the house at midnight to meet him. He'd had a bottle of Two Buck Chuck. Giggling and passing the bottle back and forth, they'd climbed the water tower in the light of the full moon. "In five-foot letters in green neon paint he wrote 'Trent loves Emma.'"

"Awww, that's so sweet."

"The police chief of Terrytown didn't think so."

"What's it like in jail?"

"Stinky. Luckily, I wasn't there long. My dad bailed me out, but he also forbade me to ever go near Trent again."

"And like a good little girl, you obeyed?"

Emma felt her face flush. "They watched me like a hawk. But one day I did sneak out to see him, but then…" she paused, remembering. But it was too painful to continue, so she said, "Then his dad got a job here in Colorado and he moved away not long after. I hadn't seen him again until today."

"Wow," Izzy said, "so how are you feeling now?"

"For one thing I'm ticked off at you. Or at least I was."

"You've forgiven me?"

"I can't stay mad at you for very long. Besides, I realized something."

"What's that?"

"My whacked-out notions about love and romance started with Trent. I poured everything into him, assuming a relationship would make me whole. I never got over that notion. I kept searching for my missing piece. There were Doug and Ryan, but nothing ever felt completely right, and the harder I tried to force things to work, the more it seemed I pushed those guys away. I think from now on I'm going to be more like you, Izz. Take me as I am or leave me alone."

"I don't have all the answers, Em," Izzy whispered. "Far from it. I keep things light because I'm afraid."

"Afraid of what?"

Izzy paused for so long that Emma thought she wasn't going to say anything at all, but finally she took a deep breath and continued, "That no one will really want me. Not for the long term."

"C'mon, Izz, of course someone will want you. You're gorgeous and fun and—"

"A long-term relationship with a quality guy is about more than just having fun. I don't think I have the staying power, you know? I mean what role models do I have? My mom's been married four times. Dad is on his third wife. I haven't a clue what makes a good relationship."

"Ah, hell, Izz, none of us do."

"Except Bianca and Madison. I can't believe how quickly they found guys they're so sure about."

"I would be skeptical, too, but they both seem very happy, and Thomaz and Jake are great guys."

"Why can't we find guys like that?"

"Beats me," Emma sighed.

Silence fell between them. Outside the tent they could hear the snap of embers settling in the fire pit, smell the smoky scent on the air.

"Do you think that the reason you never felt complete with Doug or Ryan is because you were supposed to be with Trent?" Izzy ventured.

"You mean he's my soul mate?"

"Yeah."

"I thought you didn't believe in soul mates and destiny and true love and stuff like that."

"I didn't think I did, either. Until Bianca and Madison. They make it seem so possible."

"Yes." Emma nodded in the darkness, felt something tighten in her chest. "They do."

"But you believe in that stuff, right?"

"I used to. Now I'm not sure."

"You know what I heard once?" Izzy asked.

"What's that?"

"That your soul mate isn't the one who makes your life easier, but rather the person who challenges you to be your best self."

"Interesting theory."

"Neither Doug nor Ryan challenged you, Em. You picked guys who were just like you. You wanted someone you could get along with. You avoided conflict."

Izzy was right, but Emma didn't want to tell her that.

"I bet that after Trent, you went out of your way to avoid guys who scared you in favor of guys who just went along for the ride."

"Are you sure you didn't go to college and sneak in a few psychology classes?" Emma asked.

"Hey, I spend my days analyzing my cartoon character, Cherry Forever, maybe I absorbed a thing or two about relationships in the process."

"Great, now we're taking love advice from your fictional alter ego." Emma laughed.

"Too bad we've got this bet going on." Izzy sighed. "Otherwise you could see where this thing with Trent is destined to go."

"I, for one, am grateful for the bet. It'll keep me from doing something I might regret later."

"Hmm," Izzy said.

"Hmm what?"

"I don't think anyone would ever regret having sex with Trent."

That, Emma thought, was an understatement if she'd ever heard one.

THE NEXT MORNING, Emma crawled slowly out of bed sorer than she'd ever been in her life. Every muscle in her body ached. Even her teeth ached. She got up just before dawn, unable to stay lying on the cold ground one second longer.

Izzy was sound asleep, curled up in a ball inside her sleeping bag. Emma was a true morning person and she loved being up before everyone else. She woke up cheerful and wide awake, something none of her boyfriends had ever appreciated.

Except for Trent. He'd been a morning person, too.

She took a bath towel and the eco-friendly soap she'd bought specially—she had read *some* of the brochure—from her backpack, eased from the tent, careful not to awaken Izzy, and slipped outside. She found her canteen and took a long drink, then used the toilet facilities that had been set up.

Stretching, she wished for a shower, but the closest she was going to come to one was to wash in the river. No one else was stirring so she padded down to the water. A whisper of orange and purple lights pushed at the edge of the eastern horizon and the air smelt crisp and clean and natural. This made up for all the aches and twinges tugging at her body.

The water was going to be frigid, no two ways about it. She draped the towel over a nearby bush, took off her pajamas and placed them alongside the towel. Wearing only her undergarments and armed with a bar of soap, she steeled herself and stepped to the water's edge. Although generally she was the type to ease gradually into things, when it came to cold water, the best course of action was simply to dive in and submerge. Once you had the shock over with, your body quickly adjusted.

She jumped in, grateful that the sensor in the sex-toy undies was waterproof. No one could accuse her of having sex.

The shock of the icy water took her breath and a shiver drove through her like a spike. She forced herself to stay under with only her head breaking the surface and in a few seconds the stunning effects of the water lessened.

When she was so numb she couldn't really feel the cold anymore, she stood up and began soaping up her arms. A half moon shone down on her, glistening whitely off the ripples in the river. And she felt utterly at peace.

WEARING NOTHING but a towel wrapped around his naked waist, Trent padded barefoot down to the river, intent on washing up. Then he saw the woman standing in the water. Instantly, he knew it was Emma. She'd always been a morning person just like him.

He stopped dead in his tracks and stared at her, fascinated.

Lust cemented him to the spot. Instantly, he was aroused.

He should call out to her, alert her that he was coming to the water's edge. He should move. Make noise. Do something. Instead, he merely fisted his hands and kept staring.

Just a second longer. Then he'd say something. That is if he didn't ejaculate all over himself first.

His mouth dropped open in delight as he watched her. Transfixed. There was no other word for it.

She had her back to him and at first, he thought she

was naked, but then she turned and the moonlight caught her full on, and he realized she was wearing some kind of white, diaphanous garment. It wasn't a nightgown and it was more than underwear. It had a thin bodice and a skimpy little white G-string panty that was practically non-existent when wet. But there was something else, as well. A thin white belt that went around her waist and dipped low into a V in the front.

Somehow, the fact that she was not completely nude was even more erotic. She soaped up, splashed like a water nymph.

He was breathing fast and his cock got tighter and harder and he could not move.

God, he'd forgotten just how gorgeous she was. So ripe and lush and feminine.

And if Trent didn't have her, he was going to die.

EMMA THOUGHT she heard a noise and raised her head. There standing on the path to the water was a wholly masculine figure wearing nothing but a white towel around his waist. And that towel was jutting straight out over a very impressive penis.

Trent.

She smiled and allowed her gaze to track from his face to his bare chest. God, she'd forgotten just how handsome he was. If anything, he looked even better than he had ten years ago. He could have doubled for an underwear model, that's how fabulous his torso was with those sinewy muscles and a masculine tuft of hair running from his nipples to where it disappeared beneath the stark white towel.

That's when Emma realized he'd apparently been standing there for quite a while watching her. "Come on in," she called. "I was just about to get out."

He sauntered down to the water's edge, his penis bouncing like a proud soldier on parade.

Okay, this was a mistake. Why had she told him to come down? She had a mad impulse to bolt and swim away into the darkness. He was giving her that naughty-boy grin she remembered.

Fine. All right. She could handle this like an adult. She started for the shore just as he reached the water. She was so busy staring at his broad, muscular chest and trying desperately not to look down at his steel rod of an erection that she slipped and stumbled.

"Whoa there," he murmured huskily and put out a hand to catch her.

His hand felt warm, the water cool. Emma stared into his eyes, pinned to the spot by his strong, steady gaze. He moistened his lip with the tip of his tongue and she realized she was simultaneously doing the same thing.

"I've got my balance, you can let go of me now."

He took away his hand and with it the heat. Instantly, she felt cold.

"Could you hand me that towel please?"

He handed her the towel, his eyes eating her up.

"Thank you."

"You're welcome."

The conversation was trite but the exchange between them was not. Every bit of sexual energy she possessed snapped in the air from her to him. She wrapped the towel around herself and they stood, their eyes locked. And if Myrtle hadn't chosen that moment to come stumbling out of her tent, Emma couldn't say what might have happened.

4

CHASTITY BELT. Trent couldn't get over the fact Emma was wearing a chastity belt. He'd seen it up close and personal. Why was she wearing a chastity belt? The question had been driving him nuts all morning.

Trent grinned to himself. He'd like nothing better than to spring open that little lock—with his teeth.

She sat at the front of the raft as far away from him as she could get. He wished she wasn't wearing that bulky life jacket and helmet so he could appreciate the sweet curve of her back, but whatever. He still had a good image of her in his mind, standing waist-deep in the water in the pale light of breaking dawn, her sheaf of wheat-colored hair brushing against her spine. He gulped. Felt himself harden again. Okay, this was nonsense. He'd never been so out of control before. But Emma wasn't just any woman. She was the first woman he'd ever had sex with. The first women he'd ever loved.

And ten years ago, he'd blown it. Big time.

He still remembered the night they'd gotten arrested. The fear in her eyes. Her father's anger when he'd come to spring her. The dark conversation her old man had had with him out of Emma's earshot, telling him that his daughter was too good for a bad boy riff-raff like him. And Trent had agreed, never talking to her again.

He'd given in to his insecurities. Secretly, he'd thought the same thing as her father—that Emma was too good for him. She was smart and loved books. She'd been class valedictorian, whereas he'd been a C student at best. She had ambitions. He'd had no direction. Her family was upper middle-class and his family lived in a trailer park.

That same week she'd learned she'd been accepted into Yale. He wasn't going to college. He didn't want to keep her from achieving her full potential, especially for a loser like him. It still hurt to remember how much pain he'd caused her, though he'd believed it was for the best. He closed his eyes, recalling how she'd slipped from her father's house in the middle of the night to see him. But when she'd tapped on his bedroom window, he'd cruelly told her to go away, that she'd been nothing more to him than a fling. She'd started to cry and then fled, and he'd had to fist his hands and bite the inside of his cheek to keep from going after her.

But what was done was done. It had played out the way it had and no amount of wishing or hoping could change it.

He steered the raft down the river and took a deep breath. He'd finally found peace here and he wasn't going back to the city. Emma was a nice blast from the past, but that's all she was. He was an outdoorsman from Colorado. She was a librarian from New York. You couldn't get much more opposite than that.

So why was he so attracted to her? Why had he always been attracted to her?

He remembered the first time—hell, the only time—they'd made love, the night before the water-tower incident. It had been in her bedroom on a weekend when her parents had gone out of town. Everything in her room had been decorated in pink and white, a frilly girl's room. He'd felt completely out of place, his big masculine body in that girly bed. The riff-raff mucking up Daddy's little princess.

Trent moistened his lips as the old anxiety swept through him. His self-confidence hadn't been this shaky in a very long time. Emma. Apparently her love life hadn't been so hot lately if she'd resorted to a chastity belt. Neither had his. He hadn't had a real girlfriend in over two years. He'd had a couple of casual flings since then, and while they'd satisfied him at the time, he longed for more.

A longing for Emma.

Opposites attract.

She'd been the yin to his yang. He'd been spontaneous and athletic and aggressive. She was cautious and a couch potato and shy. Or at least she used to be. From the looks of it, she'd changed. He'd changed, too. More than he should, Trent wanted to discover all the ways she was different.

Leave it alone. She wasn't for you then and she isn't now.

Yes, he should just forget about her. Forget about anything more going on between them.

That's what a smart man would do.

But when it came to Emma, Trent had never been smart.

THE HOURS passed in a flurry of activity. They ran more rapids. These more strenuous than the ones they'd encountered before. This time, Emma had learned from her mistakes and she did not end up in the water again.

They did some bird-watching with a pair of big binoculars that Trent had brought with him, taking turns looking for a rare bird that inhabited this part of Colorado. After that, they went ashore to hike a small mountain, scaling up to ten thousand feet for a beautiful view of the river below. The panorama was breathtaking. They made camp in the mountains that night, no tents this time. Sleeping near the campfire, directly under the stars. Emma had never felt so free.

In the middle of the night, she got up to relieve herself. Beyond the campfire, it was pitch-black. She'd never seen darkness this complete. It took her breath and stilled her heart. She felt at once utterly alone and completely joined with the entire universe. The stars glowed like little beacons in the vast night sky. She gazed up and saw a shooting star so bright it made her blink.

Make a wish.

"I wish," she whispered, "I could kiss Trent just one more time before I die."

"That could be arranged," came the sound of a deep-throated voice from the darkness.

Emma whirled around, but she couldn't see a thing. She heard heavy footsteps crunching on falling pine needles and twigs, smelled the sharp bite of pine, tasted the crisp night air on her tongue, felt her heart stumble headlong down a rabbit hole of trouble. "Trent?"

"Still wishing on stars, huh, Emma. You always were a romantic."

She could sense him more than see him. It was too dark to see more than a couple of inches in front of her face. And she could hear him breathing, rough and quick, matching her own erratic rhythm. "I…" She didn't know what to say so she just kept stammering. "I…I…"

It didn't matter. Trent's hands were curling around her shoulders as he tugged her into his embrace and his mouth—oh his hot, tasty mouth—was on hers.

Sensation assaulted. Heat and moisture and musky

smells. The taste of nostalgia wrapped around her tongue and it was as if they'd never been apart.

In the turn of a second they were teenagers again, kissing in the back seat of his old jalopy. One of those big old American cars of yesteryear with tons of room for making out.

Emma moaned softly and just let the past come rushing up to meet her. She twined her arms around Trent's neck, heard him groan low in his throat. "Emma," he said roughly. "Em."

It was a kiss to end all kisses. A homecoming sweeter than anything she could ever have imagined. In fact, it was so unbelievably potent she wondered if she was still in her sleeping bag, still sound asleep and she was simply dreaming of a moment too wonderful to be real.

How many times had she imagined such a reunion? A lot in the days after his family had moved away. Then less as she finished high school and went off to college. After that, her thoughts of Trent had dwindled. Mostly, she only remembered him after a romantic relationship went sour as she wondered, what if? What if her father hadn't been so rigid and judgmental. What if Trent's father's job hadn't moved him halfway across the country at just the wrong time? What if she'd defied her father's orders and written to Trent? What if, what if, what if?

And now here was the answer, with a whole new question. What if she kissed him all night long?

Emma smiled.

"What's so funny?" Trent asked, pulling his lips away in the inky blackness.

"I can't even see your face."

He slipped his arms around her waist, pulled her up tight to his chest. "But you can feel me."

No doubt about that. His erection was a slab of granite

pressing into her belly through the rough material of his denim jeans. Oh yeah, she could feel him.

"Trent, I…"

"You wished on a falling star and now you've got your wish," he said, and in the darkness his lips found hers again.

She sank into the heated wetness of him, let herself be washed away on a tide of emotions—longing, hoping, wistfulness, passion. So much passion. She'd never felt this kind of irresistible magnetism with any man before or since. He was one of a kind. Trent Colton. And he was kissing her as if tomorrow would never come. As if they could stand here forever kissing on and on into eternity.

It was a nice fantasy and she clung to it as surely as her fingers clung to his arm.

"Emma." He breathed into her mouth, her name heaven on his lips. "Emma."

He squeezed her tight and her legs went up around his waist of their own accord. Good thing she was so small and he was so big. He made her feel incredibly delicate. A fragile flower, cherished and beloved.

Then just like that, he let her go. "I can't. We can't. Myrtle and Izzy are asleep right over there."

"I know," she replied hoarsely.

"It's against my personal policy to have sex with customers."

"It's against my vow of chastity."

"What is that all about, by the way?" He chuckled. "If you don't mind me asking."

She waved a hand, even though she knew he couldn't see the gesture in the darkness. "I don't want to get into it."

"Some guy do a number on you and you swore off men?"

"Something like that."

Trent muttered a curse low under his breath. "Luckily the guy isn't here or I'd punch him out for you."

"He didn't hurt me nearly as badly as you did," Emma said. "Why did you break up with me?"

"I was a dirty, riff-raff Colton, remember? I'd never amount to anything."

"Those were my father's sentiments, not mine."

"I didn't think I was good enough for you. Your family was one of the wealthiest in Terrytown."

"And now?"

"Now you've taken a vow of chastity and I've got a business to run."

"We could get past those things," she said, not even aware she'd been considering it.

"The real question is," he said lightly, "do we want to?"

ALL THE NEXT DAY, Trent couldn't stop thinking about the kiss they'd shared in the dark, or what Emma had said. They could get past the superficial obstacles standing between them. After the trip was finished, he was free to have a relationship with her. And a vow of chastity was easy enough to forsake.

What neither of them had mentioned were the bigger differences between them. They hadn't been able to overcome them when they were young. Emma had come from a well-heeled family. He had been nothing but a C student going nowhere fast. Yes, he'd since pulled himself up by his bootstraps and made something of his life, but they were still too different. He realized it every time he looked at her. She was so sweet and innocent, even in her late twenties, even though she lived in New York City. Whereas Trent relished the rugged Colorado life. He'd become skilled out here, but he would always be out of his depth with books and society. She deserved the polished white knight on the charger spouting poetry and bringing flowers, and that just wasn't him.

He concentrated on his job, guiding them down the rapids. Today, they were hitting Grade IV white water. Not a big deal for him, but the women in his boat were total greenhorns and he'd need to keep his wits about him to make sure everyone got through safely.

Early that afternoon, he spied the landmark triangle of conifers that told him the rapids were up ahead. A minute later, they could hear the sound of rushing water. His pulse kicked up as it always did when he got to this point in the river. He loved shooting the rapids and no matter how many times he did it, it still felt like the first time. Like kissing Emma.

Even though he was fully focused on his job, Trent managed to keep an eye on Emma. He told himself it was because he didn't want her to fall into the river again, but he knew that wasn't the truth. He wanted to see how she'd react to her first real taste of white water. Would she be terrified? Anxiety bit into him. Was she tough enough for this?

A few minutes later, amid the squeaks of terror and squeals of laughter, he got a glimpse of her face and his question was answered. Emma's eyes were bright, her cheeks flushed, her upturned face splashed with water, a huge grin spread from ear to ear. She was loving it.

"Omigod!" she exclaimed after they'd passed through the thick of the rapids and his heart rate was coming down. She turned back to beam at him. "That was the most awesome thing in the world! Way better than any roller coaster."

"Fantastic!" Myrtle exclaimed.

"It rocks!" Izzy raised her arms over her head.

Trent smiled. "I'm glad you liked it."

"When's the next batch?" Emma asked.

"Not for a couple more miles."

She looked disappointed. "Darn, I'm ready to go again."

He felt flattered and had no idea why. It wasn't as if he'd invented the rapids for her entertainment.

No, but you showed them to her. He'd shared his world with her and she'd responded with more enthusiasm than he'd thought possible.

Trent observed Emma again and his stomach did a wild little dance.

And that's when he realized he was falling in love with her all over again.

"WHITE WATER, totally cool, who knew?" Izzy said when they made camp that evening.

They pitched the tents early and went fishing, catching enough trout for a huge dinner. It was the most delicious fish Emma had ever tasted. Myrtle had taken a walk and Trent had volunteered to wash the dishes. Emma sat beside Izzy, watching the sunset and feeling utterly blissful. How long had it been since she'd been this happy?

"This is the best vacation ever," Emma said. "Thank you for forcing me into it."

"You're welcome," Izzy replied.

"I didn't give you much credit. I thought you were trying to throw me in Trent's path so you could win the bet."

"Me?" Izzy acted affronted, but Emma knew not much fazed her friend. "Would I do something like that?"

"You would."

Izzy's dancing eyes met hers. "I did." She grinned. "So how you doing on the chastity thing?"

"My lock is still clicked."

"Mine, too."

"We could just call it a draw," Emma invited.

"Are you suggesting we abandon the bet?"

Emma shrugged.

"What about Bianca and Madison?"

"They're already out. This is between you and me."

"If you want to throw in the towel," Izzy said. "Go right ahead."

"But you're staying chaste?"

"Right up to the bitter end."

"You really want to win this bet, don't you?"

"Yup."

"Why? I mean I know you need money to pay off your credit card, but what you'll make off the bet you spent on this vacation."

Izzy pursed her lips, but said nothing.

"Did something happen?"

Izzy's eyes darkened and if Emma didn't know better she would have sworn she saw tears gleaming there. But Izzy didn't cry easily. She was the toughest person Emma knew. "Izz?"

"It was Eric."

"The guy you had a fling with last summer?"

Izzy nodded.

"What about him?"

"After we broke up, I realized I had a pattern. I go to bed with guys too soon. Usually on the first date. After that, I bail quick."

"You don't have to. You could change that."

"Which is why this bet means so much to me. I need to prove to myself that I can forgo sex. That I can have a friendship with a guy before I end up in the sack with him."

"It's really that hard for you?"

She shrugged. "I'm highly sexed, what can I say?"

"Not that there's anything wrong with being highly sexed, but do you think there's an emotional reason behind why you go to bed with guys so soon? Are you actually afraid of exposing your heart?"

"Like I said, I have no good role models."

"So you beat romance to the punch and take intimacy out of the equation right off the bat and just go straight to the sex."

"In a nutshell."

Emma blew out her breath. "Some people might say you're the smart one. Romance is complicated."

"Like what's going on between you and Trent?"

"All I can say is that it's good I'm not alone in the wilderness with him," Emma replied. "If I was, you'd win that bet hands-down."

"Hmm," Izzy said and a pensive look came over her face. "Is that so?"

THE NEXT MORNING Emma woke to find Izzy already gone. That was a first, Izzy was such a night owl. She stretched, got a drink from her canteen and then walked to the river. That's when she noticed the raft was missing.

She raced up to the tents. One for Myrtle, one for Trent and one for her and Izzy. Izzy's backpack wasn't in the tent. A sense of panic fluttered in her chest. What had Izzy done?

Maybe she'd talked to Myrtle.

Emma went to Myrtle's tent. "Myrtle, you awake?" she called. When Myrtle didn't answer, Emma poked her head inside, saw that the other woman's backpack was gone, too.

"What's going on?" Trent asked, standing outside his tent, yawning and scratching his head.

"Izzy. She's taken Myrtle and the raft. They left."

"Slow down." He made a calming gesture with his hand. "They probably just went fishing."

"With their backpacks?"

"Why would Izzy and Myrtle go off without us?"

"So that we'd be stranded alone together and Izzy could win the bet. Myrtle probably figured it was romantic."

"You're serious?"

Emma nodded.

"Well, Izzy's plan isn't going to work. I've got the satellite phone. I'll just call David and he'll come get us." Trent disappeared inside his tent but a moment later Emma heard him exclaim, "Dammit!"

He popped back out of the tent.

Emma's gaze met his. "She took your satellite phone, didn't she?"

"She did."

"Which means she probably took my phone, too. So what are we going to do now?"

"I don't imagine she'll leave us stranded out here forever. Do you?"

"With Izzy?" Emma shrugged. "Who can tell?"

5

"WE HAVE two choices," Trent said after they'd eaten breakfast.

"What's that?"

"We can either start walking—and I've got to tell you it's a very long hike to the nearest main road…"

"Or?"

"We can just stay here until Angie and David get worried when I don't check in and drive out looking for us, or until Izzy develops a conscience and comes back."

"Don't hold your breath on that last one," Emma mumbled, repacking the breakfast dishes. "So, if we decide to wait, what are we going to do to pass the time?" she ventured, slanting a coy glance his way.

Trent wriggled his eyebrows. "How important is that bet to you, anyway?"

Emma started laughing. "Not at all."

The next thing she knew, she was in Trent's arms.

"Emma," he breathed.

She kissed him with all the passion that had been stewing inside her for the past ten years.

He threaded his hands through her hair. She slipped her palms up under his shirt. His skin was so warm and hard. Just like the rest of him. She inhaled deeply, smelling his wonderful outdoorsy scent. The heady aroma of nature's cologne—water, sunshine, man. Their tongues glided over and around each other. Playing, teasing, cajoling. How long she'd waited for this without even realizing she'd been waiting.

"I'm not casual when it comes to relationships," Trent said. "I want you to know that."

"Neither am I."

"This means something. You mean something to me."

"Ditto."

"Emma," he said, "I feel like I've been in a long deep-freeze just waiting for you to come back into my life. I didn't acknowledge it until now, but somewhere in the back of my mind, in the bottom of my heart I kept hoping that one day…"

"Me, too," she whispered. "Me, too."

She didn't care about the stupid bet anymore. Let Izzy win. Izzy needed to win. All she cared about was Trent. As soon as they returned to civilization, she'd tell her friends she was out of the bet.

He swung her into his arms and carried her into his tent, arranged her gently down on top of the sleeping bag.

"Um, do you have protection?" she asked belatedly. She hadn't even thought about it.

"I have a condom in my wallet. But just one, so we have to be frugal."

She gave him a wicked smile and licked her lips. "Ah, but there's other things we can do."

"What kind of things?"

"Well, for starters remember the thing you did to me when we first made love?"

"As if I could forget."

"We could do that again and I could do it back to you."

"Woman," he said. "I like the way you think."

He reached for her fleece top and pulled it over her head, then he took off his own and tossed both garments to the side of the tent. He made short work of the rest of her clothing—including the chastity belt—and then tucked into foreplay with a serious intent. He kissed and nuzzled, nibbled and sucked. Her lips, her chin, her nipples. Ah, her raw, achy nipples that tingled at his touch, telegraphing a message of urgent desire straight to her womb.

For hours they played. He traced his fingertips over her sensitive belly and she mirrored his movements, giving back as good as she got. He murmured sweet everythings into her ear, telling her how beautiful she was and in detail describing everything he wanted to do to her. His naughty words lit her up inside and her hands roved over his body, feeling every sensitive masculine body part.

Finally, when they were stripped bare and naked, his erection burgeoned, thick and heavily veined.

"My, my," she cooed. "You're bigger than I remembered."

He blushed and that blush did a strange thing to her heart. He was shy with her. This big, commanding man. Then Emma saw that Trent was trembling.

"What's wrong?" she whispered.

He shivered from the top of his head to the bottom of his feet. "I've never felt anything so overwhelming, Emma. It's clogging me up. I want to be with you more than I want to breathe."

"You're with me, Trent."

"I'm worried I won't live up to your fantasies."

She grabbed him by the hair, forced him to look her in the eyes. "You could never, ever disappoint me."

"What if the sex is really bad?"

"It won't be," she said. "It's with you. Our first time was magic. This time will be, too."

"Emma," he murmured and trailed his hand over her bare skin again, tracing enticing little circles all the way down to the where her thighs met.

She spread her legs and let him in, his fingers tickling her. She grew even wetter, which was a total surprise because she hadn't thought that was possible. She arched her back, wanting him, begging him with her body to give her what she longed for, what she desperately needed. "Come inside me, Trent. Take me now."

"Not just yet."

"You love torturing me."

"I do at that." He grinned. "But in the very best way."

Lowering his head, he pressed his lips to her bare belly and kissed his way back up to her straining nipples. She quivered.

"Does that feel good, sweetheart? Tell me what you like."

"Good." It was all she could manage.

He flicked his tongue over one straining bud and then oh-so-lightly bit down. Razor-thin shards of pleasure spread throughout her breast. She moaned.

He smiled and kept at it. His mouth sucking, his tongue teasing, fingers tickling. Brilliant. He'd honed his technique in ten years.

He left her nipples and traveled downward. He spent a little time at her navel, producing crazy, erotic ripples in her belly that undulated all the way down into her sex.

When his lips reached her straining, hungry clit, he stopped short of touching her with his tongue. His breath was hot against her tender flesh, igniting her beyond comprehension.

She arched her hips again, trying to bring his mouth and her clit into contact, but he moved with her, keeping his mouth just out of her reach,

"Please," she gasped. "Stop tormenting me."

Then at last, he relented and buried his head where she wanted it, his mouth touching her innermost lips.

Every muscle in her body clamped down hard and she had to bite the inside of her cheek to keep from moaning.

"Go ahead." His voice lowered, went huskier. "Moan all you want. There's no one around to hear you but me. Wait until you see the things I'm going to do to you."

Things? What things? A dozen stimulating images tumbled through her head.

While he suckled her clit with his mouth, he slipped a finger into her slick, wet sex. Her moist walls sucked at his finger, gripping and kneading him in rhythmic waves, pulling him deeper and deeper into her.

She existed in the delicious void, floating without a body. She was total sensation. She hovered on the brink of orgasm but he would not let her fall over. A steady strumming vibration began deep in her throat and it emerged as a wild moan.

"Please," she begged. "Please."

"Please what, babe?"

"Please make me come."

He gave her everything, then. His tongue danced, his fingers manipulated. She let go of all control. Let go and just allowed him to take over. It seemed he was everywhere. Over her, around her, in her, outside of her. He was magic. He was amazing. He played her with accomplished precision. She was his instrument, tuned and ready.

"More." She thrashed her head. "Harder."

He gave it to her just the way she asked for it. Pumping his hand into her while his thumb pressed her clit.

"Come, babe, come," he coaxed.

She came. Exploded into great, writhing pleasure. Sating her soul for the first time in ten long years.

TRENT WOKE some time later and immediately reached for Emma. Her body was so lush and warm. He couldn't stop touching her. How had he gone so long without touching her? She smiled dreamily at him.

"Hello, Mountain Man," she whispered and snuggled close to him.

He couldn't believe he was with her again. That they were back where they'd started all those years ago and the feelings bubbling inside him were richer, purer than they'd ever been before. He kissed the top of her head, inhaled the scent of her hair. He cherished this moment, understood it was the beginning of something great.

Whoa, wait, don't get ahead of yourself. You don't know if she's as invested in this as you are.

"This morning was wonderful," she said, "even if every part of my body aches."

"There's one part of my body that's aching for you."

Her eyes lit up as her hand traveled south of his waist. "Pervert," she said as her fingertips lightly grazed his rock-hard erection.

"It's all your fault, lady," he growled low in his throat.

Quickly, she flipped over and straddled him, her hot little fanny resting on his abdomen, his penis bouncing against her bottom. She was amazing. All sunshine and smiles.

She leaned forward to place a kiss on his lips and he closed his eyes. *Please don't let this be a dream.* Because that's what this felt like. His deepest dream come true.

He wrapped his arms around her waist and held her steady. "I want you, Emma."

He kissed her again, tasting, savoring it, savoring her. She was one hell of a woman, his Emma. She was soft and sweet on the outside, but on the inside she was tough and determined. He admired her so much.

The heat throbbing in his solar plexus began to grow, radiating outward and upward, encompassing every part of him, making a home in his heart.

This was the missing piece of the puzzle. His Emma. If he'd only known, he would have gone in search of her. Kept them both from floundering, making mistakes.

But maybe they'd been destined to be apart. To make those mistakes and learn from them so when they hooked up again they'd be truly ready for each other. The idea comforted him, made him feel as if everything had been destined all along and it was falling into place just as it should. Fanciful thoughts and he was not a fanciful man, but he thought them nonetheless.

Her hands were all over him, moving, roving, exploring. Finding sensitive nooks and crannies that he hadn't even known were sensitive. His hands were doing some exploring of their own, tickling, teasing, caressing, kneading. Soft sounds flew from her lips and he realized he was making a few noises of his own—pleasure, delight, joy.

He felt the fire of it race through him, burning, a forest fire of need. She was frantic, too, yanking at his hair, rocking her pelvis against his.

She pressed forward, thrust one pink nipple in his face. "Suck me."

He didn't have to be told twice. Slowly, he suckled that sweet tip, pulling it into his mouth, nibbling lightly with his teeth until she moaned and ground against him harder, faster.

His penis surged, yearning to be joined with her. He left her with a kiss to retrieve the condom. Only it wasn't in his backpack. So much for being prepared for anything. What was he going to do? He had to have her or go mad.

"Emma," he said. "We gotta stop. I don't have that condom after all." He felt like a teenager.

"I'm on the pill," she said. "And I've been to the doctor. I'm healthy. How about you?"

"Yes, I get checked regularly."

"So we've got nothing to worry about."

"Are you sure you want to take that step?"

"Trent," she cried. "Take me."

"You got it, babe," he lifted her up and settled her down on his erection.

Her gasp of breath tightened his abdominal muscles. It felt so good to slide into her unsheathed. Bare flesh against bare flesh. No rubber between them.

"More," she urged.

He let her slide down as far as she could go, taking him in to the hilt. She let out a strangled moan of pleasure and began to move over him, her tight little box a vise around his penis. He felt his own muscles tighten and helplessly he began thrusting hard into her.

"Trent, Trent, Trent," she said his name like a chant.

He could feel the orgasm building, bigger than the night before. He couldn't tell where she began and he ended. They were just one. Writhing in ecstasy together. They clasped each other, their bodies covered in sweat.

The rhythm took hold of him, primal. Destined. The two of them. Into each other so deep there was simply no getting out. Not that he wanted to get out. Bliss. Pure bliss.

With a bulldozer of an orgasm pulsing through his cock.

In one long, hot moment they hung suspended, staring

into each other's eyes so they saw nothing else, felt nothing else. Rising, converging, coming.

The shudder shook his body. Wrapped around him hard and squeezed at the same time he felt her jerk and shiver.

Their pants were airy gasps, barely breathing at all. Their skin was slicked. Their bodies melded.

One.

And then he remembered what he'd written on the water tower in neon-green paint.

Trent loves Emma forever.

THEY DOZED after that, neither one of them wanting to get up and break the spell. Both luxuriating in the memories they'd just created. Perfection.

"I could live here forever," Emma said as Trent peeled an orange and fed her tangy sweet slices.

"You wouldn't have said that a few days ago."

"A few days ago I hadn't found you again."

"Emma," he said. "As soon as we get back to base camp, you and I need to do some talking."

"About what?" she asked, munching on the orange.

"About what this means. You live in New York, I live in the Colorado wilderness. And we both love where we live and our careers."

Emma crinkled her nose. "Do we have to think about that right now?"

"Not now," he said, "but soon."

He was right and she knew it. Long-distance relationships were difficult, and he loved this place just as much as she loved New York. She couldn't imagine him living there. He was a wilderness man through and through. And she was a girly-girl who needed her creature comforts.

You did pretty well without all that girly-girl stuff on this trip.

Yes, but this had been a vacation. What was fine for a few days would quickly grow old for a lifetime.

A lifetime.

She looked at Trent and her heart flipped. He was the one. She knew it in her heart. He'd always been the one.

But she'd twisted herself around for men for so long, trying to be what they wanted her to be in order to make the relationships work and because of that, the relationships hadn't worked. She'd learned from Doug and Ryan that you couldn't be something you weren't. At least not for very long.

"What are you thinking about?" Trent asked.

"I'm thinking what a fabulous lover you are." She hugged him.

"Don't be evasive with me. You were frowning and I could see those little cogs in your brain whirling. Talk to me. What are you thinking?"

"I'm thinking I don't want this to end."

"Me, neither."

"So where do we go from here, Trent? Our lifestyles are as opposite as opposite can be."

"I know."

"I could try to change, but I used to do that in every relationship I was in. Twist myself into a pretzel until I didn't recognize who I was anymore. The only time I didn't do that was when we were together before."

"We're together again, so why can't you be yourself with me?"

She swept her hand at the tent. "This isn't the real me."

"Maybe you're not giving yourself enough credit. I saw how you were out there on the river. You were magnificent, Emma. And you looked so happy. I take a lot of people out here and I can tell when someone fits and when they don't. You fit."

Did she? Maybe she was changing. But how would she know if that was the case or if she was just trying to be what Trent wanted her to be?

"You're right, let's not talk about this now. Let's just enjoy the rest of our time out here," she said. "We'll re-evaluate when we're back in civilization."

It had been a fun adventure, but as a lifestyle, she couldn't see it. But was she going to let Trent get away simply because she wasn't a wilderness woman at heart? She looked at him and her stomach tugged. Surely, there had to be a way.

"I used to work in the city," he said. "Houston."

"Oh."

"I hated it with every fiber in my being. The noise, the crowds, the pollution. I spent three miserable years there before I finally wised up and moved back to Colorado."

"Why did you move to Houston in the first place?"

"To be with a woman."

"There's good things about the city."

"There are," he agreed, "and I enjoyed those things. Just not enough."

They looked at each other.

"Oh, Trent," Emma said. "What are we going to do?"

He never answered the question because David's SUV came driving down the mountain trail, horn honking.

They were rescued.

THEY ARRIVED at base camp just before nightfall more exhausted than they'd ever been in their lives. Izzy and Angie and Myrtle came out to greet them and help them inside. Then Emma went off to the locker room to shower and change clothes, Izzy following at her heels.

EMMA TOOK her purse from the locker and wrote her a check for $500. "Here you go, Izzy, you won the bet fair and square."

Izzy held up her palms, shook her head. "It wasn't really fair. I put you in front of Trent and I knew nature would take its course. You've loved him since you were seventeen. Then I stranded you in the woods. All dirty pool. Keep your money."

"How did you get Myrtle to go along with it?"

"She's like you, still a romantic at heart. She couldn't resist helping me play cupid."

Emma met Izzy's eyes. "How did you know I was still in love with Trent?"

"Remember that night at the club?"

"I remember. I haven't had a hangover like that in years. It was right after Ryan dumped me."

"Well, it might have been right after Ryan dumped you, but all you could talk about was Trent. How you were afraid he was the love of your life and you'd lost him forever."

Emma wrinkled her nose. "I said all that?"

"You did."

"I don't remember that part."

"Well, I do and I used it to my advantage."

"You were crafty enough to use it. More power to you." Emma pressed the check at her. "Please, take the money. You won the bet. You stayed celibate when we all lost it."

"Yeah," Izzy said, "but you've all got great guys and I'm all alone."

TRENT TOOK Emma to the airport to catch her flight back to New York. Since the trip had gotten cut short because of Izzy's maneuverings, Izzy had gone home early and Emma and Trent had spent the remainder of her vacation in a quaint bed and breakfast in downtown Durango making love for hours on end.

It was killing Trent to have to let her go, but he knew she had to come back to him on her terms. She looked scared and sad and shaky. So he just took her hand and held it as they sat in his SUV outside the terminal gate.

She had to run from him. Just like she'd done ten years ago when her father had forbidden her to see him and he'd pushed her away.

But this was different. She was older now and could make her own decisions. She'd be back. He knew it in his heart of hearts, and yet it was difficult, letting her go, trusting that she would return.

He got out, helped her with her luggage, walked her to the checkpoint, kissed her cheek. "I'll be waiting," he said.

I'll be waiting.

Trent's words echoed in her ears all the way to New York. This had all happened so fast and yet it felt so right. Why was she hesitant? What was she afraid of?

Emma had the answer to that one. She was afraid she was romanticizing the relationship. That it wasn't really as shiny and wonderful as she thought. That's what she was afraid of.

Trent.

She couldn't stop thinking about him, but she was determined to try. She had to be sure that what they had was real and not just some overblown fantasy. Her mother called and asked her to dinner, so she went, driving upstate to Terrytown, driving past the high school. Remembering the places she and Trent used to go.

"Mom, Dad," she said at the dinner table after they'd eaten.

"Yes?" Her mother asked. "Have some more pot roast, honey."

"Do you remember my first boyfriend, Trent Colton?"

"My, yes," her mom said. "He was a very handsome boy."

"He got her in a lot of trouble," her dad grumbled.

"He's got his own company now," Emma said.

Her father raised his head, surprise in his eyes. "No kidding?"

"Where'd you hear that?" Her mother passed her a basket of yeast rolls.

"He was my tour guide on my white-water rafting trip." Her hands shook. Her stomach knotted.

"Isn't that something?"

Emma stared at her father, feeling all the old pain freshly. "Why didn't you like him, Daddy? He might have been a little rough around the edges when he was a teenager, but he's a wonderful man. Why did you break us up?"

Her dad met her gaze. Sadness, regret, lingered in his eyes. "You want to know why I broke you up?"

She laid down her fork and knife, suddenly short of breath, her chest tight with emotion. This was it. Everything finally out in the open. "Yes, I would."

"You were eighteen, much too young for feelings like that." He paused. "I did what any responsible father would do and told him he wasn't right for you, and that he should stay away if he knew what was good for him. And for you."

"Oh, Dad."

Her father cleared his throat. "I saw the way he looked at you. I read what he wrote about you on the water tower in neon-green letters. I hadn't seen anyone that in love since I fell in love with your mother. It was too much, too fast. I was afraid you'd give up on Yale, on your future."

Emma couldn't believe what she was hearing. "You broke us up because he loved me?" Her hands trembled and sorrow welled up inside her at what they'd lost.

"Your mom and I got married too young. Neither one of us got to have any freedom before you and your sisters came along. I wanted you to have what we never got to have. Freedom and the opportunity to discover yourself."

"Honey," her mother added. "You have to understand, we figured if it was meant to be, you'd find each other again."

She silently processed this as the kitchen clock ticked off the tense moments.

She could hold on to her anger and blame her parents, or she could recognize the gift they'd tried to give her, even though she didn't understand it.

The past was gone. She couldn't get it back. What mattered now was what she and Trent had found in the present. They'd both learned and grown from their mistakes. He'd gotten over his insecurities and she could release her hurt and resentment.

She smiled then, loving her parents, forgiving them, and letting go of their mistakes. And just like that her mind was made up. "Then it's really meant to be. The minute we laid eyes on each other it was as if ten years just fell away. Mom, Dad, I'm moving to Colorado to be with Trent."

"YOU'VE BROUGHT ME to the ends of the earth to live," Emma said to Trent when she walked into the office of Wild West Adventure Tours.

He pushed away from the desk and got to his feet. "That didn't take you long."

"I went back to Terrytown."

"Oh?"

"And I saw my parents."

"Oh." His tone flattened.

"They like you."

"You told them about my company."

"Well, yeah, but it turns out they really liked you all along."

Trent frowned. "I find that hard to believe."

"It's true. They were just scared we'd end up with their life. Married too young with too many kids too soon, so they warned you off. But I'm not them, and this is my decision."

Trent stalked across the floor, scooped her up in his arms, hugged her tight. "You were my first and I..." He paused, swallowed. "I want you to be my last."

"Oh, Trent." She didn't mean to cry, but sweet tears of joy slid slowly down her cheeks.

"Don't leave me hanging here, sweetheart. Is that a yes?"

In answer, she stood on tiptoes and cupped the sides of his dear face with both palms and kissed him with a fervency unlike any other.

And they both knew in their heart of hearts it was truly meant to be.

Epilogue

One year later

"WHO WOULD HAVE EVER suspected a year ago that a chastity belt would change all of our lives?" Izzy asked.

The friends were at Jackdaw's again on a Thursday night, celebrating Emma and Trent's wedding on Saturday.

Bianca St. James Santos just smiled a sly smile and placed a hand on her rounded abdomen. Her baby, Thomaz Junior, was due at Christmas. Her husband, Thomaz, sat beside her, a protective arm around the back of her chair. Bianca was now working for Thomaz as his vice president and right-hand woman. They'd just flown in from their home in Rio and were staying at the Manhattan apartment they kept for when business brought them to New York.

Jake and Madison were holding hands under the table. On Monday after Emma and Trent's wedding, he and Madison were headed to Belize on an orchid hunting expedition. Jake had a ring in his pocket and he was planning to propose to her in a field of orchids. Just the day before, his old friend Joe had called him from the Greek Isles where he was on an around-the-world cruise. Sounding happier than he'd had in years, Joe told him about the special woman he'd met on the trip. "Love," Joe had said, "is the biggest adventure of them all." And Jake knew he was right.

Emma leaned against Trent, her head on his shoulder. He calmed her in the midst of the crowd and noise. She couldn't believe how quickly she'd grown accustomed to the quiet wilderness of Colorado nor how deeply she'd fallen in love with the serenity of the mountains. Trent leaned over to kiss her forehead. "Do you miss New York?'

"No," she murmured, "not at all."

"Let's have a toast." Madison raised her glass. "To Thomaz—for designing the ultimate lingerie."

"I second that," Jake added.

"To Thomaz," Emma echoed, her hand on Trent's knee.

"We owe you big time." Trent nodded and raised his glass.

They toasted Thomaz and then everyone cast a glance at Izzy.

"Hey, don't give me pitying looks, people. Your little chastity belt helped me most of all." Izzy grinned.

"How's that?" Emma asked.

"It's taught me self-control, and with the money I made off you guys, I paid off my credit-card debt."

"But you didn't find anyone to love out of the deal." Bianca made a sad face.

"Oh, I wouldn't say that."

"What do you mean?" Madison asked.

A sly expression crossed Izzy's face. "Hunter and I have been dating."

"Oh, Izzy," they all exclaimed in unison.

"So how's the sex?" Emma asked and giggled when Trent tickled her in the ribs.

"I don't know," Izzy admitted.

"What do you mean you don't know?" Bianca blinked.

"We've been seeing each other for three months and tonight's the night." Izzy crossed her fingers. "Right now, as we speak, we're playing Catch Me if You Can."

"And I caught you," said a deep masculine voice.

They all turned to see a handsome blond man stride over. He slid his arms around Izzy. "Honey, I've gotta tell you, that chastity belt is killing me."

"Amen!" Everybody at the table laughed.

"I don't suppose I can be Cherry Forever," Izzy said, referring to her cartoon alter ego.

"Izzy!" came the unanimous cry.

With that, more toasts were made, more food was eaten, more hugs and kisses shared. Then one by one the couples said good night and went home, each believing that they had, in their own way, won the bet and received the sweetest reward.

* * * * *

COMING NEXT MONTH

Available September 28, 2010

REQUEST YOUR FREE BOOKS!

2 FREE NOVELS
PLUS 2
FREE GIFTS!

HARLEQUIN®

Blaze™

Red-hot reads!

HB10R

*See below for a sneak peek at
our inspirational line, Love Inspired®.
Introducing HIS HOLIDAY BRIDE
by bestselling author Jillian Hart*

Autumn Granger gave her horse rein to slide toward the
town's new sheriff.

"Hey, there." The man in a brand-new Stetson, black
T-shirt, jeans and riding boots held up a hand in greeting.
He stepped away from his four-wheel drive with "Sheriff"
in black on the doors and waded through the grasses. "I'm
new around here."

"I'm Autumn Granger."

"Nice to meet you, Miss Granger. I'm Ford Sherman,
from Chicago." He knuckled back his hat, revealing the most
handsome face she'd ever seen. Big blue eyes contrasted
with his sun-tanned complexion.

"I'm guessing you haven't seen much open land. Out
here, you've got to keep an eye on cows or they're going to
tear your vehicle apart."

"What?" He whipped around. Sure enough, mammoth
black-and-white creatures had started to gnaw on his four-
wheel drive. They clustered like a mob, mouths and tongues
and teeth bent on destruction. One cow tried to pry the
wiper off the windshield, another chewed on the side mirror.
Several leaned through the open window, licking the seats.

"Move along, little dogie." He didn't know the first thing
about cattle.

The entire herd swiveled their heads to study him curiously.
Not a single hoof shifted. The animals soon returned to
chewing, licking, digging through his possessions.

Autumn laughed, a warm and wonderful sound. "Thanks,

I needed that." She then pulled a bag from behind her saddle and waved it at the cows. "Look what I have, guys. Cookies."

Cows swung in her direction, and dozens of liquid brown eyes brightened with cookie hopes. As she circled the car, the cattle bounded after her. The earth shook with the force of their powerful hooves.

"Next time, you're on your own, city boy." She tipped her hat. The cowgirl stayed on his mind, the sweetest thing he had ever seen.

*Will Ford be able to stick it out in the country
to find out more about Autumn?
Find out in HIS HOLIDAY BRIDE
by bestselling author Jillian Hart,
available in October 2010
only from Love Inspired®.*